"A Ghost?" Ian Said Disbelievingly.

He sent her what he hoped was a very sharp look.

Quinn set her teacup down and flattened her hands on the white linen of her slacks. The English certainly had a way of saying very little and implying quite a lot. "Don't you read any of your background literature? I've sent reports to the head office. Mad Mary's the reason nobody's lived here in eighty years. Come on, Mr. Matthews, you're English."

"So?"

"So...the country's lousy with ghosts."

"You don't seem very impressed. Most Americans would be wild-eyed."

"And most Americans haven't lived here for six months," she replied.

Most Americans, Ian thought, didn't have such beguiling pink lips or such large, dark eyes. If he was going to do his job, he'd have to work fast. Because seducing Quinn Rutledge wasn't part of his orders....

Dear Reader:

Welcome to Silhouette Desire! What a month this is, with six sinfully sexy heroes from six sensational countries featured in our *Man of the World* program. You'll be finding out all about these tantalizing men between the covers of six romances written by some of your favorite authors: Linda Lael Miller, Lucy Gordon, Kathleen Korbel, Barbara Faith, Jennifer Greene, and BJ James.

By now I'm sure you've noticed the portraits of our heroes on the covers of each *Man of the World* book. Aren't these hunks handsome? I simply couldn't decide which hero I loved the best, so I decided to just love them all.

And don't miss the special letter from the author in front of each book. These talented women have taken a little extra time to compose some words to you, describing how they chose their hero and his country.

So thrill to the sensuous love stories in *Men of the World*. From the United States to Europe to the hot desert sands, the books are about six heroes you'll never forget. Please don't hesitate to write and tell me what you think of this exciting program *and* of Silhouette Desire. I'm always more than happy to hear from our readers.

I know you'll love *Men of the World*. Happy reading!

Lucia Macro

Senior Editor

KATHLEEN KORBEL

A FINE MADNESS

SILHOUETTE *Desire*

Published by Silhouette Books New York

America's Publisher of Contemporary Romance

To Sally and Carole, my favorite Anglophiles and
arbiters of good taste. It's the comfy chair.

SILHOUETTE BOOKS
300 East 42nd St., New York, N.Y. 10017

A FINE MADNESS

ISBN: 0-373-05668-0

First Silhouette Books printing October 1991

Printed in the U.S.A.

KATHLEEN KORBEL

lives in St. Louis with her husband and two children. She devotes her time to enjoying her family, writing, avoiding anyone who tries to explain the intricacies of the computer, and searching for the fabled house-cleaning fairies. She's had her best luck with her writing—from which she's garnered a *Romantic Times* award for Best New Category Author of 1987, and the 1990 Romance Writers of America RITA awards for Best Romantic Suspense and Best Long Category Romance—and from her family, without whom she couldn't have managed any of the rest. She hasn't given up on those fairies, though.

A Special Letter From Kathleen Korbel

Dear Reader:

I was born and raised in St. Louis, which is a five-hour car trip from any other major city. Is it any wonder I've always had the wanderlust? People and other places have always fascinated me. I read everything I could about them as a child, and was able to visit them as an adult. Travel has become a family addiction.

Last year we visited a good friend in Cornwall who gave us an unforgettable introduction to his country. I loved the English with their sense of order, their earthy humor, their gracious hospitality. What I loved the most, though, was their possessive pride in a species that they seem to specialize in—the eccentric. When my editor asked me to set my *Man of the World* in England, I couldn't resist the temptation to share those lovely eccentrics with my audience. So, with apologies to every level of English society, with whom I share my gentle fun, I'd like to welcome you to the home of Daphne du Maurier, the gothic romance, the Poldarks. Welcome to Cornwall, to England, with all its history, its special flavor, its eccentricity.

Sincerely,

Kathleen Korbel

One

Ian Matthews arrived at Hartley Hall in a foul mood. He'd set out that morning from Yorkshire already tired and frustrated, picked up a headache in a blinding rainstorm near Birmingham and added a sore hip when he'd stopped to change a tire in the shadow of Wells Cathedral. And that was before he'd had to battle the back roads of Cornwall.

He was in no mood for this trip. In no mood for this assignment. There were other places he needed to be right now, anxious, unstable places where his expertise could be put to better use.

"You understand how it is, old boy," they'd apologized when assigning him. "A most necessary duty. One that might suit you quite well at the moment."

The problem was, he damn well did understand. Just out of hospital after yet another operation, he carried with him an unreliable leg and the residual dizziness from the anesthetic. Annoying, familiar, temporarily too debilitating for the hard work.

So he was relegated to a bucolic two weeks in a pile of stones out among the gorse and terns, while his understudy took over his primary duty. Bloody hell. Maybe it was time to give in and settle down, as he'd been hearing all weekend.

And maybe donkeys flew.

Ian was already past the old stone gates before he saw them. Pulling the Lotus to a gravel-crunching stop, he gingerly backed the car up the one-lane road, trying his best to see past the eight-foot hedgerows. All of Cornwall was like this, a patchwork of fields and serpentine roads bordered with mammoth hedgerows. Yorkshire at least had the decency to have stone fences a person could see over.

He'd just about managed the tight turn into the drive of Hartley Hall when he felt the car give a familiar lurch. Ian knew what it was even before he felt the seat beneath him list like a ship.

"Bloody hell," he muttered, resting his throbbing forehead on his hands where they gripped the wheel.

It was the spare, and he'd been too anxious to get going to fix it. Now it hissed from around a length of fallen barbed wire. Oh, well, nothing for it now but to trudge on. Opening the door, he grabbed the roof and levered himself out of the bright yellow sports car.

Overhead, the clouds were low and heavy with rain. No doubt just waiting for him to reach the middle of the moor the owners of Hartley Hall called a front park before opening up. Bending over to reach into the passenger seat, Ian pulled out the tie he'd carried along, at the same time loosening the one he wore. From Guards tie to old school tie. Deeper into the character of the moment, an officious creation close enough to his own officious self to easily pass muster.

Knotting the tie with efficiency born of years of practice, he took a quick assessing look at his attire, the best Saville Row had to offer. Perfect again for the part. Then pulling his garment bag carrying the rest of his wardrobe for his role, he turned to limp off toward the house.

A quarter mile precisely from the road, the house rose in solid squares and battlements from the Cornish moor, the myriad mullioned windows glinting dull pewter in the flat afternoon light and the sea sullen and silent far below. The style was Tudor, all gray stone and squared turrets, with early-nineteenth-century wing additions. Actually a much more pleasant place than Ian had envisioned, compact and proportional, with a well-landscaped lawn and a circular pond out front.

Not a raindrop in sight. Counting his few blessings, Ian limped on up the steps to the front door.

The ornamentation was definitely Victorian. Wrought iron, ornate and as homely as a Lancashire farmer. Ian couldn't decide which of the overdone animals clinging to the front wall was the doorbell. So he tried the rooster and promptly discovered his mistake. He fell right through the floor of the porch.

"Bloody *hell!*"

It could have been worse. He landed on his garment bag. His hip screeched once, and his head grazed the stone that lined the odd hole. His stomach lurched with sudden queasiness, the residue of that damned dizziness, and then righted itself.

He looked up the sides of the twelve-foot pit and cursed again. A few years ago, he could have scaled the smooth sides in minutes. Now, however, he was stuck. And, of course, the rain chose then to fall. In torrents. Right on him.

"Hey, up there, somebody get me out of here!"

He blinked. Then he wondered whether he was hallucinating. No sooner had he yelled than a head materialize against the flat gray light above him.

"I say, Alistair," it said from the most beguiling pink lips, its large dark eyes betraying a combination of surprise and humor at finding a man perched on his luggage at the bottom of her hole. "It looks like we've found another one."

Quinn Rutledge wasn't sure whether to be angry, amused or confounded. There was certainly enough for her to do around Hartley Hall without having to play fireman to a hapless British executive. Those booby traps, for example. She knew there were probably half a dozen more, all still undiscovered after all these years, that she was going to have to unearth and defuse before the paying public began to arrive a month from now. There were the curtains for the library that had been misplaced somewhere between London and Bath. There was still plastering and painting and stocking. And now, Heritage House Limited, whose name graced all her paychecks, had sent a corporate executive for her to baby-sit.

A wickedly good-looking executive, she had to admit, even limp and dripping from his run-in with the elements. Sitting in his bedraggled suit, sun-streaked hair pulled back with impatient fingers into lush order, he boasted aristocratic bones and enigmatic gray eyes that beckoned with just a hint of darkness beneath all that wry pragmatism. His chin was solid, his nose just a touch off plumb and his accent straight off the playing fields of Eton. He also had a limp that wasn't from the fall, and a collection of crows-feet at the corner of his eyes that aged him.

If it weren't for that limp, she would have had him neatly buttonholed and conveniently dismissed as just another variety of the Right People School of Controlling Bodies—an English cousin to the Eastern Seaboard species she'd grown to know and despair of with such intensity.

But he bore that limp with an elegant stoicism she'd never seen on executives before. He had calluses, too, hard calluses she'd felt beneath her palm when she'd shaken his hand. Calluses no country gentleman should have known how to acquire. And a dark knowledge in those devilish gray eyes that intrigued her.

"Heritage House promised me a free hand," she objected over the tea Alistair had insisted on supplying before checking on their surprise visitor's car. "After all, Hartley Hall is a bit more difficult to restore than the average country house."

Mr. Matthews looked up from where he was still brushing away long-disappeared dirt from his trouser leg. "Then I'm to assume that thing on the door isn't a tourist attraction?" he asked, his eyes sparkling with wry humor.

Quinn couldn't help smiling back, even though she knew she shouldn't. "That's one of the problems I've told Mr. Bagwhite, at corporate headquarters, about," she reminded him. "Mad Mary had a penchant for practical jokes. Even with the research we've done, we're still unearthing some of them."

Mr. Matthews sent her another sharp look from under those cultivated eyebrows. "Mad Mary."

Quinn set her teacup down and flattened her hands on the white linen of her slacks. "Don't you read any of your background info? Mad Mary, the original Countess of Thorn, the reason nobody's lived here in eighty years."

The English, Quinn decided, really had the art of the elevated eyebrow down to a tee. It was something Americans could take lessons in. For instance, with the quirk of only one small muscle, Mr. Matthews managed to convey an enormous amount of polite skepticism. Quinn imagined he saved his vocal chords quite a bit of wear and tear with the trick.

"Come on, Mr. Matthews," she objected instinctively, still fighting the smiles he provoked. "You're English. The country's lousy with ghosts. Surely you can't be so amazed that Heritage House managed to bag one here."

His own smile was telling. "You don't seem terribly impressed. Most Americans would be wild-eyed."

She had to laugh. "Most Americans haven't lived with Mary for six months."

"Smashing vehicle!" Alistair announced enthusiastically as he stormed back into the parlor. "Lotus, what?"

Quinn flinched as the retired colonel slammed the door behind him and strode into the little study where the fireplace crackled merrily against the pervasive chill. Alistair entered any scene like the military man he still considered himself, bristling with efficiency, bawling with tradition and brimming with opinions. Which, of course, he naturally assumed everyone wanted to hear.

"You've met the Colonel Sir Alistair Smythe-Smithe," she introduced him as Mr. Matthews stood to shake the proffered regimental hand. She saw the wince appear and die within the space of a blink. Saw the half weight put on that bad leg and wondered at his calm greeting. "Sir Alistair, this is Mr. Matthews. Evidently Heritage House sent him out to neutralize Mary's little surprises."

"Ripe one, that," Alistair boomed with a delighted chuckle. "Can't imagine how I missed landing on my own arse a time or two. Except, of course, that I can't abide roosters. Can't see myself yanking on one, don't ya know." Letting go, he rubbed at his hooked nose with a considering finger. "Matthews. Look familiar to me. Not the North Country Matthews by an chance?"

Here it comes, Quinn thought, wondering how she could sneak out of the room before they got to comparing pony-club experiences.

"Sussex, I'm afraid," Mr. Matthews said with a small smile. "A pleasure to meet you, Sir Alistair. I've read your account of Alamein, of course. Smashing."

Quinn fought the urge to jump to her feet. Worse than horses. War. The last thing she needed with work so far behind was the reenactment of the World War II battle of El

Alamein with Alistair as tour guide. His chest was already inflating, his great white mustache quivering with delight. Quinn had to stop this before the first salvo was fired.

"Is Mr. Matthews's luggage in the green room?" she asked.

"What? Oh, quite. Quite."

Quickly setting her cup and saucer down on the little Queen Anne table beside the couch, Quinn got to her feet. "Let me show you to your room, Mr. Matthews. I'll give you a quick tour on our way through."

Alistair stiffened in silent protest, his eyebrows quivering apace with his mustache. He had his heart set on Alamein with tea. Quinn wasn't sure, but she had a feeling that behind that carefully correct face of Mr. Matthews, he was relieved at the rescue.

"I'd be obliged for your theories on the African campaign," he said to the old man, and Quinn was surprised by a flush of appreciation for Mr. Matthews's empathy. "Maybe later, after I've done my first inspection of the house."

Alistair just nodded. "Quite."

"Alistair," Quinn added softly, a bit chagrined at her own thoughts about Mr. Matthews's generosity. "Could you take a look at the contents of the library and sketch up an idea for how to group the books?"

"Even the Kipling?" he asked. "The old girl's never been too keen on Kipling."

Quinn couldn't help but grin. "Just put them someplace where they won't be harmed when they hit the floor."

Ian suppressed a groan at the sight of the staircase across the foyer. He'd been anticipating it, because, of course, country houses were hardly famous for single-story floor plans. To Miss Rutledge's credit, she cast no more than one questioning look at his limp and took his silent assurances calmly. Ian was just glad she couldn't see how the room tended to tilt in front of him.

"Your résumé is quite impressive, Miss Rutledge," he offered, his shoes echoing across the black-and-white marble entrance hall as he followed her. "You studied renovation in Italy, I understand. Quite a privilege."

She laid a hand on the dark mahogany of the sweeping staircase, and Ian noted the slender grace of her fingers.

Ringless hands, practical hands. Artisan's hands. She was tall, comfortable against his six feet, and dark, her skin honey-toned against her deep brown hair and eyes, her scent of sandalwood and lemon, her attire tailored white linen. An exotic flower in the hothouse of England. A sharp tongue and a sharper brain. He wondered how long he'd be able to fool her.

"Miss Rutledge is my Aunt Winnie who teaches first grade," she retorted easily, stopping a step up from him and turning those deep eyes on him. "If you insist on calling me that, I won't answer."

Her scent settled on Ian like a mist and made him want to smile almost as much as her American frankness did. He couldn't imagine many professionals in England demanding first names before they'd even sat down to a meal together. "If I must call you Quinn," he answered with an easy smile, "then I expect you to call me Ian."

She tilted her head just a little, her face brightening. "Since I was going to do it, anyway, I'm glad you don't mind."

And then she turned away again.

Ian smiled and swung up after her, his hand clamped hard around the banister and his hip creaking like an old porch swing. "Bagwhite said you were from Iowa?"

She nodded, sending her dark hair dancing in a cloud around her neck. "Ottumwa." Ian saw that she stroked the banister rather than balanced with it. Her eyes lifted to take in the dark paintings that marched up the paneled stairwell, even though she probably saw them every day.

"A fair way from Milan, I assume."

"Ottumwa is a wonderful place," she assured him without turning. "Small and stable and friendly. What it isn't is very old. I've always been fascinated by old things."

She was also climbing the stairs more slowly without seeming to. A perceptive, empathetic woman. Suddenly Ian wondered why he'd objected so strenuously to coming out here.

"Cecil said I could learn a lot from your treatment of Hartley Hall. Is it your first Heritage House project?" he asked, still playing the part even though he knew her history better than she did, his eyes surreptitiously on the stairs before him.

"My first in England. And, to date, my biggest challenge."

"No ghosts anywhere else?"

"None that offered decorating tips."

Ian briefly sought out the faces in the portraits, wondering which one might be the notorious countess. "I can hardly wait to meet her."

"Oh, you will. Don't worry."

They reached the top of the stairs without mishap and turned along the east corridor. There were ladders propped against the wall farther down, and a knot of buckets huddled with rag piles and brushes alongside the blood-red carpet. Quinn stopped about halfway down and opened a door on the left.

"Each room is decorated with a different period of furniture," she explained, stepping in past him. "Yours is Jacobean."

The room was charming. Whitewashed walls, heavy dark wood. The bed was massive and intricately carved with velvet curtains flowing from its canopy, the wardrobe solid and scarred. The wiring and plumbing, so often strung right out in the open in these older renovated places, was magically invisible. A trio of arched windows overlooked the gardens that marched down the steep hill to the sea. Today the ocean and the rain sounded the same, and somewhere Ian smelled the last of the roses.

Few places to hide in the room. Only two ways in or out, and the windows would take some effort up a stone wall. Secure and empty. Except for the soft growl that seemed to be coming from behind the bed curtains. Ian instinctively stiffened.

"Copenhagen," Quinn demanded, striding past him, "what are you doing there?"

She was met by a low woof. Ian let his hand fall unobtrusively away from where he'd reached under the back of his coat.

"Copenhagen?"

"The colonel's dog."

"The colonel named his dog after Wellington's horse?"

Just then Quinn pulled the curtains back, and a black freight train on feet hurtled from the bed. Ian just had enough time to twist aside before the Great Dane's paws sent him crashing against the wall.

"Point taken," Ian conceded.

"Don't mind him," Quinn advised, scratching the big dog's ears. "He's a great coward. But he does keep your feet warm when it gets drafty. Go on," she said with a swat to the Dane's considerable rump. "Get downstairs where you belong."

The dog lifted passive eyes at her and offered one final woof of indignation before sauntering away.

Ian shook his head. "Any more surprises?"

"Not usually until the sun goes down."

Ian spent a moment walking through the room, picking up a book from the small stack on the table, smoothing a hand over the damask bedspread and volume of Spenser's poetry on the nightstand, because he knew she expected it. And because, in truth, he liked the clean quality of Quinn's work.

"I decided to make each room different," she was saying from the doorway, "because the house doesn't have much traceable history except for Mary. It didn't have any kingmakers in its pages, so no great armories or memorabilia from state visits. Family finally petered out about the turn of the century, so we don't have much of the original furniture."

Ian nodded in perfect understanding. "The Earls of Thorn," he reflected easily as he strolled back her way. "You're right about the kingmakers. I imagine you know how the first earl got his title?"

Ian found he liked that knowing smile of hers as she stood there, hands casually in her pants pockets awaiting his judgment.

"Bestowed by a grateful Henry VIII for curing the royal hemorrhoids." Her eyes danced. "It's a pity old Lord Reginald couldn't take care of the gout, too. He could have gotten a dukedom out of it."

Ian proffered a wry smile. "The flower of English manhood."

She grinned back, her head tilting again, just a bit. "Hey, he did more good than most of those pirates buried in Westminster Abbey."

Ian chuckled, his perusal of the room forgotten, his hand around the serpentine bedpost, his attention completely on Miss Rutledge. "I imagine that's not an observation you make around Sir Alistair."

She rolled her eyes and leaned her hip against the doorjamb. "Not if I don't want my bags dumped out a window at high tide." Her eyes softened suspiciously at mention of the old man, and Ian liked it. He liked the way she stood, her body supple and easy, as if she refused to be impressed or intimi-

dated. He liked her smile, a quick flash of teeth and eyes, like
a door swinging open into a room of sunlight. So refreshing,
so honest.

"Would you, uh, like to change?" she asked suddenly, and
Ian realized that for the first time she looked uncomfortable.
Her gaze faltered, shifted, and Ian wondered what he'd given
away.

He straightened himself, and took a second to consider the
sorry state of his clothes. They were damp and itchy and uncomfortable, and he hadn't noticed until she'd broken contact.

"Yes," he admitted, looking back up at her, wondering just
what he thought he was going to do here. "I can meet you
somewhere for the rest of the tour, if you'd like."

She ducked her head a little, and Ian thought he saw a faint
stain on her neck. "We can try the chapel next, then. I'll, uh,
meet you in fifteen minutes. Beyond the east drawing room."

And they stood there, the two of them, as stiff as children
meeting at their first party, as uncertain as new lovers. Ian
fought the urge to reach a hand out to where that soft blush
crept up her skin. She turned away and he almost asked her
back. But he'd been trained too well. Instead of reaching out
to her, he stepped back. Shoved his hands into his pockets.

"I'll be there."

He was about to reach behind him for the door, intent on
closing her out, on closing himself safely away, when she
turned to him. She opened her mouth and then, suddenly, her
eyes. She was looking over Ian's shoulder.

Ian's reflexes were the best, but this time he never stood a
chance. Before he could move, the heavy oak door slammed
into his back like a battering ram, pushing him right at Quinn.
His choices were to grab on to her or fall on his face. He
grabbed on to her. And then he fell on his face.

Two

"Um...excuse me."

It was all Quinn could manage with the wind knocked out of her. Ian had landed right on top of her, his weight mashing her against the floor. The slamming door still echoed faintly down the hallway, and down in the front foyer, Copenhagen barked. Quinn lay flat on her back trying to get a breath, trying to get her mind to work as fast as her heart. Trying to quell the sudden chills racing through her.

"Sorry," Ian mumbled in her ear, the whisper of his breath sending shivers down her legs. His face was in her hair, his body stretched out over hers, his arms still around her.

Quinn couldn't imagine what she should do next. She couldn't believe what she wanted to do. Her heart was thundering, and it certainly wasn't from Mary's latest surprise. She actually fought the urge to turn her face to his, to nuzzle the rich gold of his hair.

"No...no problem," she managed, acutely uncomfortable. "I'd really like to move, though, if it's all the same to you."

He didn't budge. Quinn could hardly feel him breathing against her. "In a moment. Do you mind?"

She turned her face toward him. "I beg your pardon?"
She'd been in England too long. Back home it would have
sounded more like, "What the hell do you mean, do I mind?"
But then she realized how tight his voice sounded, and remembered that limp. Questions bubbled up and were shoved
ruthlessly down. It just wasn't polite, and if she'd learned
anything about the English, it was their obsessive need to be
polite.

"No," she obliged instead, trying to relax a few muscles.
"No problem. Anything I can do?"

She couldn't believe she was being so calm. Here she was
lying on the floor in a strange man's arms and they hadn't even
had supper together yet.

"Thank you, no."

Quinn wasn't quite sure what to do next. Her own arms were
still around Ian's back, and she could feel the quiver of taut
muscle. She smelled wood smoke and heard the rasp of his
breathing. She was certain he could hear her heart. She sure
could. Those curious little chills still raced up and down her
back, multiplying, snaking along her limbs.

"Your leg?" she ventured carefully, eyes rigidly to the ceiling molding where Antique Ceiling White had been untidily
splattered against Old Ivory.

"Mmm."

"Feel free to curse," she suggested diffidently. It was certainly something *she* was considering.

He actually smiled. Quinn could feel it against her cheek.
"Wouldn't be sporting, now, would it?"

Quinn chuckled. "I wasn't aware we were on a playing
field."

It took him a second to make up his mind. His voice wasn't
quite as robust as the colonel's when the old man let loose with
the odd oath, but Ian's repertoire was at least as impressive,
leaving Quinn with the impression that he'd also spent his
share of time in the military. Either that or he was an ardent
soccer fan.

"Better?" she asked without moving.

"Oh, much."

Quinn fought the urge to stroke that rich soft hair that tickled her cheek. She considered curling her arms just a little
tighter around that rock-solid back.

The thought died stillborn. Without warning, Ian pushed himself up to a sitting position. She stared at him, stunned. Considering the fact that he'd evidently been disabled enough to keep him from moving out of a strange woman's arms for what had seemed like at least an hour, he looked pretty damned composed. His face was a bit pasty, but his eyes sparkled with the most annoying humor. And Quinn was still lying on the floor with the smell of his hair in her nostrils, wondering why she should resent his moving.

"Need a hand up?" he asked, reaching over.

Quinn shook her head, furious at her breathlessness. "No, really. This is a great angle to check some of the trim. You have marvelous recuperative powers."

Ian dipped his head in acknowledgment and retrieved his hand to lean on, his back against the wall. He actually looked comfortable, as if that were the position he'd meant to assume all along.

"Stiff upper lip, you know," he offered with a wry smile.

Quinn heard Copenhagen barking again, closer now. It would be just what she needed to have Alistair top to the stairs to find her supine in the hallway with one of the corporate honchos. Pulling herself up to a sitting position across from Ian, she considered the faint sheen of perspiration on his forehead.

"Mind a question?" she asked.

Ian smiled again, and Quinn felt it to her toes. "Old cricket injury," he obliged easily.

Quinn actually snorted. "Don't be silly. What kind of injury can you get in a game where you don't even get a white uniform dirty?"

His eyebrow did that slow dance again. "Depends on whether you're playing like a gentleman or not."

"In that case," Quinn retorted, "you should get along with Mary quite well."

He motioned to the now firmly shut door. "Does that happen often?"

Quinn took a quick look herself, but she was much more used to Mary than Ian. Mary had never once raised the hackles on the back of Quinn's neck. Not the way they were now, as if they were warning her away from something. Something dangerous. Something delicious.

"Actually," she said instead, turning back to him with some determination, "you must have done something to really make her mad. I've never seen her make an appearance until everybody's safely tucked in."

"What? Rattling chains, screams, floating apparitions?"

Quinn grinned and shook her head. Let him explain it to her after he'd missed his tenth straight night of sleep. "No," she said. "Not really. But I think you're going to have to experience it for yourself."

His nod this time was brisk and efficient. "Ready, then?" he asked.

Before Quinn had the chance to ask for what, he was on his feet. She looked up a bit dumbly to find his hand once again outstretched.

"I'd like to at least get into a clean change of clothes before the old girl goes after me again," Ian explained.

Quinn gave up and just took hold of his hand. His pull was easy and strong, not a hint of discomfort marring his classic features. Stiff upper lip, hell, Quinn thought. The way this guy healed he should have been a football player.

Then he smiled again. "Your hair smells wonderful, by the way."

Quinn froze. He still held her hand in his callused one, and he looked down on her with those crystal-gray eyes. And Quinn, who had spent the majority of her life avoiding complications just like Ian, found herself enchanted.

"Thank you. Uh...the chapel in fifteen minutes then?" *I'll be the one praying for sanity.*

He threw off a vague gesture back to the bedroom. "As long as you're sure the sink doesn't explode or anything."

Quinn grinned. "We've already defused the booby trap in the bed. You're safe."

"Your time is running out."

"Running out?" Ian echoed, his head in his hands as he bent over where he sat on the side of his bed, the phone receiver pressed against his ear. "I just bloody well got here."

Damn this weakness. He'd barely made it back in the door before his knees had all but buckled. His head was buzzing so loudly he could barely hear his caller.

"They've decided to move up the schedule," the woman informed him in particularly abrasive tones, as if she considered it all Ian's fault. Which she probably did, knowing her. "Evidently the threats are making the delegates a bit uncomfortable."

At that Ian's head came upright, his forehead suddenly creased. "They still haven't managed an identification?"

"None. My sources in CID say that they're taking them so seriously that they're moving the meeting up by a week to prevent having the location discovered."

Ian laughed. "I wouldn't take odds on it. This place is still a bloody mine field."

"Exactly why they've chosen that site. Nobody will expect them in a country house that hasn't even opened for business yet."

"I'm not talking about wallpaper and a staff," Ian protested, pulling out a handkerchief to wipe away the perspiration that slid down his temples. The tea he'd drunk was sloshing around his stomach like the bilge water of an old ship in a storm, and he felt clammy as hell. Damn it all anyway, just what had he accomplished tightening the screws in his leg if he couldn't stand on the damn thing?

"Just get us a reliable layout of the place," she snapped. "The blueprints are most confusing."

"So's the layout," he countered. "It seems that the original owners had a penchant for practical jokes, and not all of them have been located. I was good enough to point one out within seconds of my arrival."

"But that house is Tudor."

"And it has a ghost who doesn't seem to care for interlopers. She could probably wreak enough havoc on the conference without having to worry about any outside help."

"Ghost," came the derisive reply. "My dear boy, you were under anesthetic too long."

"Leila, my dear old thing," he retorted, stuffing his handkerchief impatiently away, "I'd be more than glad to give you a demonstration. I'm telling you that Uzis and C4 might very well be superfluous."

"The layout," she retorted with exaggerated patience. "Just get it. And be sure to locate all those little surprises so no one falls in the wrong hole trying to scale a wall."

Leila wasn't one for lengthy goodbyes. Ian heard a click and found himself holding a silent receiver. His scowl was thunderous. "My pleasure," he snarled, and then slammed the receiver back into place.

He took one more swipe at his forehead, thankful at least that this last episode of dizziness was passing, and got up to change. He didn't have much time to get his information and get back out before the very astute Ms. Rutledge found out exactly who he was and what he wanted from her.

The family chapel was simple, pristine and elegant, an original Elizabethan structure with white paneled walls and original stained-glass windows that shattered the sun into a million jewels across an uneven stone floor decorated in epitaphs.

Quinn wasn't exactly twiddling her thumbs as she waited for Ian to show up. She'd slipped into a jumpsuit and gone back to work on the carved mahogany altar rail they'd found at the fall antique market in Paris. Balancing the delicately carved wood in her lap, Quinn planed and measured the rail to fit with an eye like a jeweler's.

And thought of the intrusion of Ian Matthews.

Executives. She didn't need executives looking over her shoulder. If they wanted to send help, they should send a thatcher. If they wanted to learn lessons, they should just listen to her advice. If there was one thing Quinn couldn't abide, it was interference.

If there was one thing she had no patience for, it was the social posturing of the Right People. She had no time for well-placed men who saw life in terms of schools and clubs and last names. She'd made that mistake once and lost three very frustrating years of her life. She didn't intend on traveling that particular path again.

That was the problem, of course. Not who Ian was, but what. Privileged, upper-class, well educated. A carbon of her past sins.

"Splendid, isn't it?"

Quinn hadn't heard the door open. Seated cross-legged on the stone floor with the rail in her lap, she looked up to see Ian standing on the opposite side of the twenty-foot room, door latch still in hand, his head back to take in the glowing late-afternoon light that showered the echoing room.

Instinctively she scowled. His attire was just what she expected, right down to the scuffed handmade brogues. Tweed, corduroy and cotton, the natural fibers of the country gentleman. And of course the obligatory tie. Old school, old club, old regiment. Instant identification with his own kind, wishing desperately to be a better kind and seeing money and prestige as his only way up.

Just like her ex-husband, Jason.

She should know better. She did know better. She'd managed to hold off an Italian count and two French restoration experts since that single unsuccessful experiment with marriage. She'd convinced an Irish art appraiser of his ill manners with a medieval brass bed warmer to the back of the head. Surely she could hold off one English bean counter.

"Old school?" she asked, fighting a new set of chills. His gray eyes were ghostly in that light.

Up went that eyebrow. "Pardon?"

She motioned with the screwdriver she'd picked up. "Your tie. Old school?"

His hand rose to caress the faded stripes. "Club."

Quinn nodded and turned back to her work. "Ah."

He couldn't seem to surprise her at all. Except, of course, for that sudden heat she'd stumbled over in his eyes back in his bedroom. The overwhelming feeling that he'd been about to reach out to her. He'd seemed almost as surprised by it as she. Almost as disconcerted.

Almost.

But then, as she'd said, she knew better.

The best defense was concentrating on her work at hand. One good look at her dedication usually cooled any inconvenient ardor. Quinn bent back to the rail, penciling in the exact position of the hinge before attaching it. "The chapel was originally built in 1540 and dedicated to St. George and St. Patrick," she lectured briskly, her eyes on her task. "To the right of the altar is a secret staircase linking the chapel with the priest hole behind the earl's bedroom. The earls, evidently, were secretly Catholic for quite a while."

Ian's smile was wry as he walked over to run his hand along one of the kneelers that were lined against the wall. "I wonder how many chambermaids made their escape through the chapel,'' he mused.

Quinn couldn't prevent a grin as she slid the pencil behind her ear and picked up the screwdriver again. ''The thought had occurred to me. The stairs were a lot more worn than I figured a priest or two would warrant.''

His shadow fell over her. Quinn wasn't surprised. That faint wood smoke had preceded him, mixing with the fresh smell of shavings from the very old wood. For some reason, Quinn's hands were damp where they held the hinge and screwdriver. She couldn't quite line either up properly.

''What did the chapel look like before?'' he asked.

Quinn couldn't help glancing up, her head tilting instinctively. ''Like this.''

Ian took another considering look. ''Even the windows?''

Quinn gazed up at the sharp blues and blood-reds of the medieval windows high over her head.

''We found them in the priest hole,'' she said, her eyes and voice softening. ''In perfect condition. Evidently they couldn't bear to sell them. They were Mary's favorites.''

Ian leaned his elbows on the scrolled pulpit and leveled surprised eyes on Quinn. ''You like her.''

Quinn met his eyes, her hands quiet against the warm wood in her lap. ''I sympathize with her. This is her home, and her family kept selling it off and changing it on her. She didn't like it.'' Quinn shrugged. ''They disappointed her.''

Ian's eyebrow did that little dance again, this time betraying suppressed humor. ''She told you that?''

Quinn's scowl would have sent half her workmen scurrying for cover. ''It seems to me I wasn't the one on his face in the carpeting just a while ago, Mr. Matthews.''

Ian bobbed his head in acquiescence. ''I've just never seen anyone so conversant with a ghost before—at least not unless that person was sitting in a tent wearing a turban and several yards of necklace.''

Quinn shook her head in frustration. ''No wonder she slammed the door on you. I'd be careful of wandering off alone, if I were you.''

''I'm not about to pull on that ornament again, if that's what you mean.''

Quinn forbore allowing triumph to taint her smile. ''I've yanked on that rooster by mistake at least six times.''

He let his eyebrow do his talking.

Quinn turned back to her work. She lined up the hinge again, the brass gleaming dully in Ian's shadow, the wood soft and dark in her hands. She could still smell Ian just next to her, could hear his soft breathing in the high, echoing room. It was just enough to distract her.

She sighed and set everything carefully back down. "What can I tell you about the house?" she asked, getting to her feet.

Not moving from where he leaned so casually by his elbows against the pulpit, Ian let his eyes widen in surprise. "Why did you stop?"

The sun sank into the startling gray of his eyes and evaporated it. Quinn saw long, honey-colored lashes, the ring of dark gray around his irises and pupils. She saw amusement, bemusement. She saw the darkness, deep down where other people might not look.

"I don't like people watching over my shoulder," she said crisply, again fighting that urge to run a hand through the now perfectly groomed head of hair that gleamed like the brass she'd had in her hands. "I can't afford to be distracted when I work."

He nodded again, just a quick tilt of the head that related everything he needed to say. "I guess I thought you'd be more of a supervisor."

Brushing the dust from her pants, Quinn shook her head. "You can't get a feel for a house from across the yard."

He straightened, gestured behind him. "Show me."

Quinn turned back to the simple altar that took up one end of the room. A block of Cornish stone, gray and smooth and dark with the fervor of centuries, it stood solid against the bouquet of color from the St. George and St. Patrick window behind it.

"When we arrived, only the walls attaching the chapel to the house had survived," she said, stepping up to stroke the altar where so much faith had rested. "To rebuild it we worked from sketches one of the family made in the early nineteenth century."

"What about the electricity?"

She shrugged. "Easy. When we carved out the stone for the walls, we simply cut a channel for the wiring, and then did a little cosmetic work with plaster. It's even easier with the paneling."

"But expensive."

Quinn turned on him, expecting the ax to fall, wondering if now she was going to get the lecture on cost containment. "Heritage House demands authenticity," she defended herself instinctively. "I try my best to maintain the illusion. It's been an enormous success at the other houses."

His smile controlled, as if he'd undoubtedly anticipated her response, Ian nodded. "What about the stairs? I would like to see them."

Quinn nodded right back. "Just do me one favor when we tour the house. Always do as I say. Mary has a lot of booby traps around the place."

"Yes," he acknowledged ruefully. "I'm aware of that."

Quinn slid her hand along the paneling next to the altar until she felt a recession. She pushed and the wall groaned. Shifting her weight, she leaned one shoulder into the section until the wall cracked. The smell of damp and mold snaked out on a thin draft.

She felt Ian approach like a warm breath. "How do we see?" he asked. "Burning torches dipped in pitch? Tallow candles?"

With a grumble and a squeal, the door finally obliged. Quinn reached around to her left and hit the switch. "Fluorescent bulbs."

Immediately the shadows melted from the stone steps that marched in a straight succession along the north wall toward the second story and the old earl's bedroom.

"How utilitarian," Ian protested, leaning past to check the sconces that spilled electric illumination.

"How safe," Quinn retorted, leading the way. "A necessary consideration when one is inviting paying guests to tour one's house."

He followed at a syncopated pace. "We don't have to let them up here."

His words echoed off the smooth stone. Far above them the priest hole was still shrouded and secret. A few lances and maces were hung along the walls for atmosphere.

"But this is one of the main attractions," Quinn said. "A real priest hole."

"Don't forget your ghost."

"Difficult to do. But there isn't anything I can do to make her any safer."

"You could exorcise her."

"Throw her out of her own house?" Quinn demanded, outraged. "Your manners are atrocious."

They'd reached the halfway point, the walls close on either side, the priest hole still invisible, the light from the chapel a faint wash alongside the glare of electricity. So, of course, that was when Mary chose to strike.

First the lights went off. Quinn instinctively stopped, the way up suddenly a frightening void. She whirled for escape, but it was too late. Just as Ian bumped into her from the step below, the door to the chapel slammed shut with a resounding thud.

"Oh, no," Quinn muttered, breaking out into a sweat. "Why take it out on me?"

Her answer was a raucous laugh that echoed up and down the steps like thunder over a river.

She felt Ian stiffen to a stop just below her, bringing their heads to the same level. "I don't suppose that's you being so amused," he ventured in a wonderfully controlled voice.

Quinn envied him his nonchalance. "Now you know why it's hard to sleep at night. I have a feeling you've just insulted Mary again."

"I apologize most humbly, your ladyship," he called, and the echo of his voice mingled with Mary's.

The lights failed to revive.

"I don't think she accepts," Quinn said. She turned around and reached for the walls on either side. Took several slow, deep breaths, desperate for orientation in the sudden blackness. When she found the walls, she tried to ease her bottom down on the stair just above her. The problem was that in the total dark, she was beset by the overwhelming suspicion that the stair had disappeared, leaving a terrible nothing so that she'd sit down and just keep tumbling into space. Quinn hated the dark. She hated close places. Until now, it had been her secret.

She had an awful feeling she was about to give herself away.

"Shouldn't we go on up?" Ian asked patiently. Quinn could feel the brush of his voice against her, could smell him again in the dark like a premonition. Vivid in the musty blackness, so that she was tempted to reach for him for stability.

"I imagine so," she answered, eyes shut, eyes open. No difference. Just Ian close enough to kiss in the middle of nothing.

Damn.

"You want to go on up?" she tried, furious to hear the quaver invade her voice.

There was a brief pause. Ian mustering his tact, she was sure.

"Are you all right?" he asked and laid a wonderfully callused hand on her arm. Stabilizing, settling, soothing.

Quinn vacillated between wanting to throw herself into his arms and push him away.

"I'm fine," she managed, blinking away quick tears of frustration. "You've just found out why I felt it necessary to put lights along the stairway."

"Claustrophobic?"

"Afraid of the dark. Ever since a tornado took the second floor off our farmhouse while I was asleep—on the second floor of the farmhouse."

Again, a heartbeat of silence. Then Ian's voice, close, gentle. "Feel free to curse."

Quinn's laughter sounded more like a sob. "I'm not sporting at all."

"I think I can survive it."

By the time she'd exhausted her own store of words, Quinn was sure Ian was convinced she'd been in the military, too.

"Better?"

She actually smiled. "Oh, yes." Sucking in a lungful of stuffy air, she curled her fingers into the solid stone. "I don't suppose you'd consider just going back to London. This is sure playing hell with my schedule."

Another pause, except this time Quinn had the impression he was smiling. "I've only been here two hours."

"Imagine what Mary can come up with once she gets up a full head of steam."

"Walk on up with me," Ian coaxed, gently pulling her arm away from the wall.

"The steps aren't there anymore," Quinn objected, stiffening.

"They are," he replied gently. "I promise."

"You go first."

It was, in the most euphemistic of terms, a tight squeeze, but Ian managed to change places with Quinn. She had to admit that there was something wonderfully reassuring about the slow steady throb of another heart pressed against her chest in that darkness. She didn't even mind that Ian seemed to find it necessary to brush his knuckles gently across her cheek by way of polite apology for molding her to the wall on his way by.

But then he was a step up, and his hand guided her into the darkness. Quinn tested the way with hesitant steps.

"There you are," he crooned with that rich accent of his, a hand under her arm, another wrapped around her hand as he climbed ahead of her. "We'll be up in no time, and then we'll lean out the windows of the earl's bedroom and look at the ocean."

"And get sick in the flower beds," Quinn retorted. Her voice tumbled down the stairs like water, disappearing into the darkness and stealing her feeling of stability. Ian never slackened his grip.

"A landing," he announced, stopping and then helping her up the last step. "Where's the door?"

Quinn wedged herself between Ian and the wall, terrified by the prospect of stepping the wrong way and ending up Silly-Putty back against the chapel door. "Should be here . . . an indentation."

She found the indentation and pulled at it, just as she had at least a dozen times before. And of course nothing happened. Quinn's failure was met by another round of echoing chuckles.

"Aw, hell," she groaned.

"That didn't sound like good news."

"Alternatives will be gladly entertained," Quinn informed him, giving the door another impotent tug. It landed her right back against Ian's chest.

He instinctively wrapped an arm around her waist to keep her from overbalancing. Quinn leaned into him, his sinewy strength easing her sense of disorientation.

"Let's sit down," Quinn suggested, the echo of that last ethereal chuckle enough for her to know that they weren't going to get this door open from the inside.

"Splendid idea."

"Then let's suck our thumbs."

"No better alternatives?"

"It's much better than crawling into a fetal position and sobbing."

"Ah, well. Yes."

Ian supposed that after spending much more time at Hartley Hall, he should at least regain some of his patience. First he'd had to sit in a deep hole for half an hour. This time it looked as if he'd be stuck at the top of the stairs for even longer. Quinn had shouted and pounded and made liberal use of a vocabulary Ian hadn't heard since his army days. And still Ian was wrapped around Quinn on the tiny landing at the top of the stairs.

Maybe waiting wasn't such a bad thing. He might not in the least mind getting to know Quinn a little better. So far he'd spent half an hour in the company of nothing but her voice, the hint of her scent, the delicious warmth of her body cradled against his. And in spite of the rigors he'd had to survive over the weekend, he'd enjoyed it immensely.

She was so bloody sharp. So bright. She felt so vulnerable curled up in his arms, her head resting against the hollow of his shoulder so that the whisper of sandalwood kept tormenting him.

If only he weren't the man he was. If only he didn't know exactly how Quinn would react when she found out. If only he weren't developing such a surprising fondness for dark, dark eyes and artisan's hands.

"Tell me a little about yourself," he suggested.

She'd been silent for a while now, and Ian suddenly realized she was trembling.

"I can't..." Her voice was small and raspy, as if forced through frozen chords. She curled up into a tighter ball, cold and shaking.

Ian had a sinking feeling that her indomitable will was about to fade on him. "I'm right here," he assured her again, instinctively wrapping his arms more tightly around her. He knew what the darkness could do to one's imagination. Monsters lurked in the dark. Enemies, poised to spring. The shapes of familiar things metamorphosed and threatened.

"I can't breathe," she rasped, ducking her head more deeply against his chest. "There isn't any room."

"They'll be along soon," he promised again, that litany a much too familiar one. "Tell me about Ottumwa."

"No...I can't think...I want to..." She lifted her head, so that Ian could almost see the liquid terror in those eloquent eyes. "Oh, God," she whispered, her hands in his, her voice tattered. "I'm trying so hard."

Ian meant to say something. He meant to comfort her, to cheer her on. But in the darkness, he was overwhelmed, too. By the warmth of her, the scent of her, the husky desperation in her voice. Letting go of her hand, he cupped her face in his palm, feeling the damp skin, the fresh splash of tears. And because he suddenly couldn't think, either, he bent to kiss her.

Ian had no proper warning that they were about to be rescued. The door into the earl's bedroom didn't even squeak as it swung open. One minute there was that total, impenetrable blackness he'd almost grown accustomed to. The next, a blistering shaft of light blinded him. There was no mistaking the military bearing of the silhouette dead center in the doorway, though.

"Oh, I say," the colonel apologized immediately. "I didn't mean to interfere."

And just as quickly, he shut the door again.

Three

"**W**ait!"

Ian almost sent Quinn tumbling down the steps in his hurry to grab the door before it swung shut again. He heard the click just as his fingers brushed stone.

"Colonel!" Quinn called, jumping up beside him. "Sir Alistair!"

The old man must have heard. Again there was no noise, just the sudden stab of light as the door swung inward to halve what little room they had on the ledge. Quinn lifted a hand to shade her eyes against the light. Ian grabbed her arm to keep her from losing her balance and edged her toward the room beyond.

"My thanks, Colonel," he acknowledged with a pat on the old man's shoulder as he guided Quinn past. "We've been stuck in that blasted hole for a good half hour."

The colonel just nodded. "Wondered where you'd gotten off to. You've very nearly missed tea."

"I guess you didn't hear Mary," Quinn offered, slipping neatly out of Ian's grasp and beyond the colonel where she could swipe at her cheeks unnoticed.

"Course I heard her," the colonel retorted with a huff as he once again shut the door. "But I believe she knows better than to think she's going to interfere with my tea."

Quinn dropped her hands to reveal a dry grin. "Of course," she agreed.

"How'd you know where to look for us?" Ian asked, thinking that Quinn looked pretty composed for being so close to collapse back in that hole. Woman had nerve.

The colonel swung his considerable attention Ian's way and frowned. "Met you before, haven't I?"

Ian turned his attention back to the old man. "Downstairs," he obliged with some bemusement. "About two hours ago."

The colonel waved off the impudence. "Of course that. Before. Thought came to me when I saw you curled up in that corner. By God, I thought, I've seen that face before. Have a memory like a lion, don't you know. You served, sir?"

Ian all but held his breath. How to lie and stay close enough to the truth. This was a man who could spot a lie faster than Mad Mary slammed doors. Pensioners like him could quote the service record of every regiment in the Queen's service. Probably spent his time in the loo memorizing *Debrett's Peerage* and digested the history of the Horse Guards over crumpets.

Ian straightened with the pride the old man would expect and named a regiment. "Greens," he obliged, lying. And hoped that lions didn't have quite the memory elephants did.

The colonel nodded, his eyes still squinted in consideration, and turned to lead the way to tea. "Copenhagen, of course."

Ian turned to Quinn for help, but she just shrugged, considering the fact that the Great Dane was nowhere to be seen. Unless, of course, he was referring to *another* Copenhagen, in which case Ian figured he'd never find out. Perhaps Ian had served there with the Greens. It was certainly possible. He had no idea in the world where all the Greens *were* stationed.

"We'll be down in a minute," Quinn told the colonel. "I wanted to show Ian a bit more of the house."

The old man turned on her, his mustache bristling in some outrage. "But the tea's getting cold."

Quinn smiled, and Ian couldn't imagine any man resisting the look. "I'm sure you'd love a pot of Earl Grey all to yourself. I'll serve Mr. Matthews and myself when we get downstairs. Just don't eat all the scones.''

Smythe-Smithe didn't say anything, but Ian could tell from the brief communion of his eyebrows that he was disappointed. Schedules upset, routine disrupted. More than that, though. Ian had the sneaking suspicion that the old man counted on Quinn's sharing his tea. Ian was going to have to make short work of the tour.

"Quite," was all the old man said as he spun on his heel and marched out of the room. "I'll be in the library."

Quinn didn't move until the sound of his footsteps faded into silence. She was still looking toward the empty door with a fond expression. "He is a dear."

Ian was thinking more of the young woman who commanded such a man's loyalty. "He's going to miss you terribly when you move on."

She turned to him, and Ian saw a bit of the cost of her work.

"He'll have the house," she said. "That's why getting one of the locals to become manager has worked out so well. They don't have just a sense of history, they have a sense of possession. This is already his home."

"And you?" Ian couldn't help but ask. "What's home for you?"

Quinn smiled, and Ian thought it looked much too wistful. "I adopt whatever place I renovate. Right now I have five homes, with friends running each one."

"Don't you want permanence?"

"I'll find it," she promised. "When I'm ready. Now, would you like to see how an earl sleeps?"

Ian almost slipped on two counts. It took him a second to restrain the urge to answer her. Instead, he redirected her. "You recover quickly," he said with a small grin.

She stopped where she stood, the faint blush on her throat all that gave her away. For a moment Ian was sure she was going to mention the liberties he'd taken. Or shared. He still wasn't certain who had come away with the most from that kiss. He knew he was in the greatest danger from it. He should be looking for chinks in the Thorn armor. Instead he was thinking of skin that smelled like flowers.

"Once the lights come on, I'm a different person," she allowed, her eyes careful and noncommittal, the message implicit.

Ian smiled. "Then the darkness isn't worth mentioning."
Her relief was obvious.

Quinn had intended the tour to be a short one. After all,
Alistair was waiting downstairs, and she hated to disappoint
him. Somehow, though, she found herself going into great
detail in every one of the rooms she and Ian walked through.

"The security system is already wired up and working," she
offered as she watched Ian run a hand over the smooth curves
of the Greek torso that took up one of the alcoves in the long
gallery. They were finally on the homestretch back toward the
library where Sir Alistair waited.

His attention on the room itself, Ian nodded absently. "All
the windows are wired, I saw. Do you have pressure sensors in
the floor?"

"It's a country house," she reminded him, "not a mu-
seum. If we used anything that fancy, we'd have the police
down here the minute some guest decided to take a late-night
stroll. Besides, the only major painting we're including is the
Gainsborough. The rest are basic eighteenth-century land-
scapes and the odd family portrait."

Ian turned her way finally. "I thought you said you didn't
have many of the Thorn possessions."

Quinn couldn't help but grin. "I didn't say it was *their*
family."

He nodded, hands in pockets again until he got to the next
statue, a bust of Wellington that was the colonel's favorite.
Again he stroked it, as if he needed physical contact to appreciate something. "Do you have the amperage for adding extra
security wiring if need be?"

Quinn couldn't quite take her eyes away from that hand—a
hand that should have been perfectly manicured, smooth and
as soft as the man. Instead she saw scars, and a little finger that
had obviously been broken in the past. It bent just a little in
toward his other fingers at the joint. And then there were the
calluses. For some reason, they fascinated her.

But then, he probably hurt himself falling off his horse
playing polo. God knows it seemed the popular thing to do.

It didn't explain that kiss, though. The sudden sweet comfort of his arms. It didn't explain her reaction to him, which
baffled her most of all.

She was still watching the sweep of his fingers down Wellington's shoulder when Quinn realized that Ian had turned to her. She hadn't even heard the question he'd just asked.

"What?" She blinked, more surprised than he by her lapse of attention.

"What would be the chances that, if needed, someone could upgrade the system? Install something more sophisticated."

"A little too late to ask for that now," she said. "You should have stopped by earlier, while we still had the wiring exposed. Why the question?"

Abruptly he looked up, and Quinn was beset by the feeling that she'd caught him daydreaming. His quick smile was disarming.

"A question raised about clients bringing their baubles and such. We just wanted to make sure they were safe during grouse season when the household is out trailing the beaters."

"Guests," Quinn instinctively corrected him. "We do not call them clients."

His eyebrow lifted. "Sorry."

She shook her head. "That's been in the last three policy statements from Heritage House. Obviously you're not reading them any better than Alistair."

"I don't always get along so well with that Malham crowd," he admitted.

"The Earl of Malham himself?" she asked, fascinated. "Or Bagwhite?"

Heritage House Limited had been founded by the Earl of Malham to preserve the family fortunes from the taxman. A corporation built around offering a sample of the gracious lifestyle the earls had enjoyed since their own induction into the peerage on the field at Bosworth. The earl's name was on the letterhead, but his son-in-law Cecil Bagwhite ran the company—with a ruthless hand, from all accounts, but very successfully. He'd managed to build it into a multimillion-dollar international concern, thereby saving the earl from having to open up the family seat to paying guests and turning the family land into an animal park to preserve the treasures housed within.

He'd also made Heritage House into a very exacting company, which was why Quinn couldn't imagine Ian making the gaffe he had. Heritage House employees served the company much as if it were the Crown itself.

"Neither," Ian admitted, his eyes still assessing the mostly empty corridor. "The earl thinks too little of himself and Bagwhite too much."

"Have you seen Malham Hall?" Her mouth was damn near watering.

Ian's smile was private, enigmatic. "Once or twice."

"I would kill to get my hands on that house. I've heard that nobody's done any renovation since the mid-nineteenth century."

But Ian was already shaking his head. "Ah, now you've just given yourself away. They'd spot you as an interloper in a minute. They could never consider letting you touch one faded chintz cushion."

"But that's criminal. How can they not take care of something so distinctive?"

"Ah, but they do consider it taken care of. They simply don't want to go changing things about. They've been collecting those odds and ends for several centuries, and they've got used to them sitting exactly where they are."

Quinn lifted a wry eyebrow at him. "And what country house did you grow up in?"

Ian's laughter was abrupt. "St. Alban's rectory. My father was a vicar. I'm the second son of a second son. Not nearly glamorous enough."

"Still old, though, I bet. Full of history."

Ian's expression was a bit bemused. "As much as anyplace else in this benighted country. You really have a passion for old places, don't you?"

They'd once again slowed to a halt, this time right alongside the original copy of the family title grant. Just as she always did, Quinn lifted a hand to the glass, as if she could feel the last echoes of Henry VIII's legendary power from the blob of indented red wax that was his signature. "An obsession," she admitted. "During the time I renovate a house, I can actually imagine it's mine. That I can walk along the halls my ancestors walked three hundred years ago, look out on the same vistas, hear the same whispers and creakings. It makes them alive again . . . and, well, mine."

"What about your own house?" he asked. "Your own family?"

Quinn looked over at him, at his well-bred looks and traditional bearing, generations of upbringing that produced an heir to a culture. And, just as she did every time she left one of her houses, she allowed herself a brief stab of envy. "My family is borrowed," she said with a bright smile. "I'm adopted."

He seemed to consider that seriously. "It makes such a difference?"

Quinn shrugged. "In day-to-day things, no. I have a great family. But I'm a historian. Only I have no history of my own."

His smile was wry. "Makes some of us ungrateful sods that we don't appreciate ours."

She rubbed a little at the glass again. "They say that people who live in the wilderness never notice the mountains until visitors point them out. Now then, anything else about the guests' baubles you need to know?"

It took Ian a moment to answer, as if he wanted to pursue another line of conversation. Finally he turned back on his way down the hall. "Do you have a repository if a lady wants to leave her sapphires while she chases old Fred into the brambles?"

"There's a state-of-the-art safe in Alistair's office," Quinn assured him. "Satisfied?"

"You are most thorough," he commended her, walking on.

Quinn just shook her head. "That's what I've been trying to tell you all along."

"And this room?" he asked, turning the knob on the door to Alistair's office.

"Oh, that . . ."

Quinn was following close on his heels when Ian came to a dead stop. She caught herself just short of rubbing her nose in his tweed. "Problems?" Quinn instinctively moved up to see.

Ian shoved her back with one hand and opened the door with the other. Quinn could see the austere furnishings beyond as the door swung inward, a wall of military books, a simple desk and leather chair, a pipe rack and a globe, the only ornate thing in the room. And, of course, Copenhagen, curled up on the rug by the gas fire. He lifted his head at the intrusion.

Ian crouched down right in front of the door, both hands spread out before him, like a mime outlining a box. Quinn couldn't figure out what he was doing.

"Do you know what this is doing here?" he asked, and his voice sounded suddenly different. Not cultured, not drawling with education. Succinct. In command.

"I don't even know what it is," Quinn insisted, trying to bend for a closer look. He just shoved her back again.

"It's a trip wire," he informed her, his hands making a return pass across the doorway.

It was then that Quinn saw what he'd spotted right away, a gossamer shimmer across the space, as if a spider had swung across the open door spinning thread behind it. From the way Ian tensed before it, Quinn was pretty sure they weren't talking spiders here.

"Do me a favor," he suggested. "Go on into the library and get the colonel. See if he has any ideas about this."

Maybe it was the mention of the colonel. Maybe he was just as curious as the rest of them. Unfortunately, Copenhagen didn't understand the concept of a delicate situation. Quinn had just started down the hall when she heard Ian let out an oath. She whirled around just in time to see him throw himself across the hall. Right on his heels came Copenhagen—straight through the trip wire.

The flash blinded her. She clapped her hands over her ears, expecting the immediate concussion of some horrible explosion. Too stunned to move, too surprised to be afraid.

But there was no explosion. No plaster rained upon them; no furniture sailed through the air. There was just the sound of Copenhagen's snuffles as he investigated the rolled-up man in the hallway.

Carefully pulling her hands away from her ears, Quinn approached Ian. This time he was the one flat on his back, and she was the one with the hand out.

"I'm beginning to think it's not me," she informed him. "I think you just like throwing yourself on the floor."

"Well, we won't be getting any photos of the old girl tonight," Alistair said.

"You wouldn't have, anyway," Quinn insisted yet again. "The last I heard, ghosts don't have enough substance to trip booby traps."

"It worked for Bronwyn Morwellan down in the village," he insisted. "She's the one who set the contraption up. I merely offered my office, since I'm usually the only one in there, anyway, and Mary's so fond of practicing her cricket bowl with my biography of Cromwell."

Quinn grinned over at Ian, who was blowing the steam from his tea. "She detests Cromwell. Laughs her head off every time that book hits the wall."

Ian rubbed the back of his neck a little, wishing his hip would let up, wishing he'd packed that tin of codeine the sister had forced on him when he'd limped away from the hospital. Wishing he were hunkered down in a foxhole anticipating mortar fire rather than this.

"The dog," he said. "How did he get in the office?"

Quinn pointed to the door camouflaged in the wall at the far corner of the room. "It connects through the anteroom to Alistair's office. Copenhagen always goes in from the library. He's usually the one that picks up the Cromwell when Mary gets mad, because she doesn't have the heart to throw anything at him."

At the sound of his voice, the big dog lifted his head from where he lay curled up on top of Quinn's feet. Ian was ready to cash it in. He wasn't even sure he was going to survive one night, much less the entire mission. He picked up a biscuit and bit into it. Sipped at his tea. Watched the glitter of reflected fire lick up Quinn's face and warm her eyes.

This was absurd. He needed to get the hell away. He didn't want to.

"Sussex, you say," Alistair said suddenly.

Ian barely heard him enough to nod.

"Family still there?"

"My father passed away. My mother lives with her sister in Blackpool."

Alistair's nose actually wrinkled in distaste. "Quite. A member of Boodles, I see. Don't approve of it at all, I must say. Allowing women in and all."

Ian was still preoccupied by the problem of his hip and the residual nausea that was making a return trip even as he tried to drown it with tea. All he could manage in return was a halfhearted grunt.

"Women?" Quinn retorted from where she was curled up in the wing chair across from Ian. "In a private club? How beastly! I must apply immediately."

Ian looked up in time to see Alistair bristling with discomfort and Quinn smiling like a satisfied cat. "I hear the food's even better back in the women's dining room," he unaccountably encouraged her.

She rested a very amused gaze on him. "Do you mean I couldn't eat at the same table with you?"

That almost made the old man apoplectic. "Now, see here," he protested, fondling his mustache as if afraid it was in danger, as well. "It's not that you wouldn't be welcome, that is to say... well, at certain places. It's just that a man's club is...is..."

"Sacred," Ian provided.

The colonel nodded emphatically. "Exactly."

"A haven from all that female bother."

"It's just... well, there must be somewhere a man can be comfortable doing as he wishes."

Quinn tipped her head to the side, that gamin look still on her face. "And exactly what is that?" she asked. "I've often wondered precisely what it is men are so desperate to do they can't do it in front of women."

"Read the *Times* from beginning to end," Ian promptly provided. "While smoking the greatest, most foul-smelling cigar he can find."

She nodded thoughtfully. "I like the *Times*," she mused. "In fact, I could probably learn to smoke a good cigar if need be. Does this include the revered waiter supplying the obligatory post-prandial cognac without being asked?"

"Naturally."

Quinn nodded. "Then that's it. I'm going."

The colonel actually glowered. "One of these days, young lady, I'm going to take you seriously."

"One of these days, Sir Alistair," she gently chided back, "you're going to have to."

He huffed a little, like a rooster resetting his feathers, and reached over to snatch another biscuit from the almost empty tray. "You've nearly distracted me," he accused, waggling the morsel at her. "And that just wouldn't do." Without waiting for the question Ian could see forming on her face, the old man turned to him and leveled the biscuit at his tie. "Know Tuffy Whalsey-Bragg? Served with him in Burma, of course. Grenadiers. His father was the Earl of Clanghan. Brilliant cricketer, master of the hunt."

Suddenly Ian was paying attention. He was being grilled. It was a game as old as the empire: school, family, social ties. But this old man was serious. And the last thing Ian needed was to fall prey to inattention and botch up his story. He didn't need this man finding out the truth. Not at all.

"Whalsey-Bragg?" he echoed with a faint shake of the head. "Don't believe I do. I don't make it into the club as frequently as I'd like. On the road so much, you know."

"Which reminds me," Quinn immediately piped up. "I've been wanting to ask. What exactly is it that you *do* for Heritage House? Security? Small arms? You've never quite mentioned."

Shelling and small arms at once. Ian had to stay alert. "Acquisitions," he replied. "I'm the one who finds those lovely piles of rubble that you've been refitting into works of art."

She tilted her head slightly. "Kind of a closed-end situation, isn't it? I mean, there are only so many viable piles of rubble still out there."

He nodded. "That's why I'm here. Making the decision about whether to go the next step and bid on some halls and such that really need the work."

"Like what?"

"Kinsale Manor in Ireland."

The minute Quinn brightened up, Ian felt relieved. He'd successfully deflected her interest. Now if he only knew his part well enough.

"But Kinsale is only a shell," she protested, even though the avid glint in her eyes betrayed her. "A victim of the English tax system."

Ian nodded. "No windows, no roof, no taxes. Yes, I know. There are several sites like that. In poor condition, but with such romantic histories that the effort at restoration might be worthwhile."

She nodded, that little tilt of the head that communicated so much. "I'll help you on one condition."

Ian couldn't prevent a smile as he took a sip of his tea. "That being?"

"That I get first crack at Kinsale."

Ian nodded. "I was hoping you'd offer."

"Humph," the colonel protested, rattling his own teacup like a saber. "I'm sure you were."

Both Ian and Quinn looked at him in surprise.

"There's something you'd like to tell me?" Quinn asked.

"There are a few things I'd like to ask Mr. Matthews, if you'd just let me. After all, girl, there isn't anyone but me to look after you."

Ian set the Spode cup and saucer back on the tea cart. Quinn seemed rather dumbstruck by the old man's words.

"Now then," the colonel continued, stroking that mustache again, his eyes sharp as small agates. "I assume you schooled in Sussex?"

"Shrewsbury, actually," Ian drawled. "Then Magdalen."

"What was your first? History?"

Ian smiled. "Political science, history, anthropology. I had brief aspirations of doing something noble."

"Excuse me," Quinn interrupted, her sharp eyes spearing the colonel. "This might be incredibly presumptuous of me, but exactly why are you questioning Mr. Matthews in my interests? Just what are my interests, Alistair?"

Alistair blinked at her as if she were a very slow child. "Why, marriage, of course."

Quinn was only a little more stunned than Ian. "Marriage?" she retorted a half octave higher. "Whatever gave you that idea?"

Again the colonel looked as if he were explaining the obvious. "Why, Mary, of course. Where have you been, girl?" Turning back to Ian, he lowered those formidable eyebrows at him. "The old girl's not only famous for her hauntings. She's also the most effective matchmaker in the entire duchy. It doesn't take a clairvoyant to deduce that she's trying to throw you two together. So, I have a few more questions, if you don't mind."

Four

That night Quinn got less sleep than usual. And not because Mary was laughing, either. That night, she hummed. "Greensleeves," of all things. Considering the fact that Mary had ended up with no fewer than four husbands over the course of her considerable life, Quinn guessed the song wasn't that much out of line. On the other hand, it didn't ease her sense of dismay any.

The colonel had been right. Mary was notorious for her matchmaking. It was said that if two young lovers met in Mary's bedchamber beneath a full moon, she'd let them know—in no uncertain terms—whether they were meant for each other. One hapless youth had been seen sailing through the night air into the front pond when his suit was rejected. But Quinn had discounted it all as just amusing local history.

Until tonight.

It made a weird kind of sense. Especially the way Mary had laughed herself blue—could ghosts get blue?—when Quinn had found herself abruptly in the dark with a handsome man. There had been workmen, artisans, architects and local officials by the score traipsing through Hartley Hall, the vast majority men, and Mary hadn't once thrown Quinn into the arms of any of them. Or vice versa. Usually she hadn't even disdained to make her presence known.

Instead she'd chosen to bestow her largesse upon the man least likely to stir Quinn's respect. A very proper, civilized executive who probably rated himself by the people he'd known in that school of his and the number of times he'd made it into the royal enclosure at Ascot.

That simply wasn't Mary's style. She'd been notorious for her penchant for rogues. She'd funded a privateer and supported Irish rebels. More than one rumor suggested that her marriage bed wasn't very sacrosanct, and that a hiding highwayman or two had helped fill the family coffers. Quinn couldn't imagine why the old lady would have picked the model of a modern corporate general to inflict on her.

Unless, as Quinn was beginning to suspect, Ian Matthews wasn't what he appeared. Unless those calluses and that split-second reaction to a booby trap Quinn hadn't even seen meant more than the tweed and pinstripes.

But was that good or bad? And why would somebody like that be buying romantic ruins for a living for a company that measured itself in the number of titles it attracted to its various hostels? A company that had interviewed Quinn over high tea to make sure she could handle herself properly in a society whose caste system was both rigid and socially deadly to the unwary.

There was no question that Ian Matthews would have passed muster. Quinn just wondered why a man who had obtained degrees in political science and anthropology, and obviously honed his physical reactions to a razor edge, would want to.

After a while, the soft spectral humming lulled Quinn to sleep. Still wondering what it was Mary saw that Quinn didn't.

"But do you think you'll be finished on time?"

Quinn sat at her desk in Mary's old music room rubbing her eyes. "It's going to be touch and go, Allison. I'm still waiting for that new thatcher to arrive, and the full license has yet to be approved for meals and liquor."

"Oh, you don't have to worry about that, dear," the woman assured her from her own Victorian-style office in London's Berkeley Square. "We do have some connections. It's just that we've booked a party for opening weekend, and I'd so like for everything to be ready.''

It was a beautiful day outside, a typical English spring afternoon. The sun glinted on the tumble of waves far below, and in the back garden, the rhododendron were beginning to send out pink and white buds. The wysteria would bloom soon, and after it the honeysuckle. By high summer, the gardens that spread out to the cliffs overlooking the beach path would be a riot of gentle color, with sweet peas, hollyhocks, lupins, delphiniums and cornflowers elbowing each other in untidy profusion. The massive oaks would shade the walks in the park, and the beech would tremble in the wind.

For the first time since she'd been traveling, Quinn yearned to be here to see them all bloom. She wanted to be able to stroll over to the stables and watch the mares grow into pregnancy, and take a few days to hike the coastal trail, right up to Tintagel. Then she wanted to curl up in a familiar room with very old, very loved furniture and rest.

Quinn rubbed her eyes again and smiled to herself. Maybe she wasn't the wanderer she'd thought. ''I can guarantee the workmen,'' she promised Allison. ''What I can't offer is a promise that we'll defuse all of Mary's pranks by then. You know we just found another one yesterday.''

Allison's chuckle was throaty and rich. ''Another falling canopy?''

''Worse. A trap door at the front entrance. And of course it was somebody from head office who fell through it. I felt terrible, especially since he had a bad leg and all to begin with.''

''From Heritage House?'' Allison retorted quickly. ''Who in heaven's name went all the way out into the wilds?''

Allison's bailiwick was interior design for the houses. The very stylish and quite unthinkably intelligent daughter of an aged duke and a showgirl, Allison was the one who conferred with Quinn on just what pieces would work in a house and who ordered all materials. Allison had been the one to pour Quinn's tea the afternoon Cecil Bagwhite had grilled Quinn in his high-pitched nasal voice.

''His name's Ian Matthews,'' Quinn said, looking out to the yard. She was facing west, so that the stables were to the side of her view. A familiar set of tweed-covered shoulders were headed that way. ''He's in acquisitions. Do you know him?''

She was going to have to head him off before he got to the paddock. The only permanent resident so far was a rogue steeplechaser the Malhams had cashiered to pasture at the far end of the universe from their spectacular Yorkshire digs. Blackie would just as soon bite as wink, and that was the last thing Ian or Quinn needed.

"Matthews," Allison mused. "Don't think so, but there's quite a crowd over in acquisitions. Lawyers, accountants, historians."

Well, that explained part of the mystery.

"What did he say he's doing there?" Allison demanded. "He should have checked with me, since you're still supervising out there."

"Said he's investigating my restoration techniques to decide whether it's worth it to buy Kinsale Manor."

Allison snorted unkindly. "You'd think one of them would simply think to read the textbook you put together after Casa DiAngelo." There was a pause, which made Quinn smile. "Kinsale?"

"That's what he said."

"Have him ring me, dear. I would like to speak with him. About channels."

"And Kinsale."

Allison chuckled. "Oh, and by the way, is the security system going to be fully operational?"

Quinn stopped smiling. "Of course, why?"

"Oh, nothing. That party we booked is a bit skittish about that kind of thing. Some pretentious great mucky-muck or another, don't you know."

Once again Quinn's gaze strayed to where the red brick of the stable block showed at the far corner of her window. This time, though, she was frowning.

"He asked me the same thing," she said. "Does he have anything to do with reservations?"

"Someone in acquisitions? Don't be absurd. I only know because the people in reservations called to double-check the security. Nothing special, they assured me. They just wanted a bit of reassurance."

"Then why would Ian ask?"

Quinn didn't even realize she'd spoken aloud until Allison answered. "I'd be happy to ask him. Do have him call."

And Quinn, who was still watching the empty corner of the stables, nodded. "I think I will."

The day was brisk enough for Quinn to don a sweater on her way out the door. Evidently Ian had thought so, too. She could see cable-knit beneath the ubiquitous tweed jacket as he leaned against the white paddock rail, one Wellington-clad foot resting against a rung and his elbows over the top. Trotting his way was Blackie himself, his ears twitching and his nostrils fluttering with soft whickers. Ian held out an apple to him.

"That's not a good idea," Quinn advised, wishing she didn't feel so much like the one out of place here. She was terrified of Blackie—ever since he'd done his best to snack on her forearm when she'd been naive enough to do the same thing as Ian.

But Ian looked so perfectly natural here, a country gentleman in his natural habitat. The breeze tousled his fair hair. The light dappled both him and the horse. Trees nodded with their infant leaves and the air was warm and fecund.

"Oh, an apple can't hurt the old fellow," he objected, never turning away from the approaching horse. Blackie slowed to a walk and edged up, his tail swishing like a brush across a snare drum. Not more than ten feet from the rail, he stopped, and his head came up. His ears went flat and then stood straight up.

Ian smiled.

"That's right, you old rogue. It's me. Now come get your bloody apple before I shove it down your throat with a stick."

And much to Quinn's eternal amazement, Blackie walked right up like a recalcitrant child, his head down in submission, and plucked the apple from Ian's hand as delicately as a duchess taking refills from the tea cart.

Quinn stared. "How did you do that?"

"You just have to know how to talk to him," Ian informed her without turning away. He was stroking the velvet muzzle Blackie presented, and the great black horse was whuffling contentedly.

"You two are acquainted, I take it."

"Old friends."

Quinn tentatively approached, still wary of the animal that stood at least seventeen hands and had teeth like the average sugarcane shredder. "I understand he belonged to the earl. Did you see him race?"

"Oh, yes." Still he stroked, the communion with the horse silent and somehow poignant.

"I've never seen a steeplechase," she admitted. "Knowing this guy makes me think it's a fierce sport."

"All-out war," Ian said quietly. "Black Pagan here won the Cheltenham Gold Cup in his prime. Quite an achievement. Quite a race."

"I wish I could have seen it."

"He bit two horses in the warm-up ring and almost threw his jockey three times before the race even started. And then he won the bloody thing by twelve lengths, and that was with a stress fracture. It was his last big race." Ian shook his head, a slow movement that betrayed more than wonder. "I had no idea he was here."

Quinn turned to say more and saw something in Ian's eyes that silenced her. Pain. Loss. Separation. She looked back at the horse, and then again at Ian, and knew that what she was seeing had everything to do with a lost passion and an injured leg.

"How long has it been since you've ridden?" she asked quietly.

Ian looked at her with a smile that broke her heart. "Oh, I've ridden. It's just quite impossible to race when you have so many screws and bolts holding your leg on."

Blackie butted Ian's arm, impatient with the lack of attention. Ian laughed and swatted at the big horse, who seemed to consider it a sign of affection.

"And where's the apple this time, you bloody beast?" Ian demanded, his voice suspiciously soft for the questionable language.

Blackie butted him in the chest.

"Not even close. Behave yourself or you starve."

The horse lifted his head and promptly nipped at Ian's hair. Quinn would have been on the ground with her arms over her head. Ian laughed again. Then he produced the other apple from a deep jacket pocket and handed it over.

"He had one of the foulest tempers and most magnificent hearts in the sport. I'm glad they're taking care of him."

Quinn chuckled. "He's had the satisfaction of terrorizing every stable boy on the north coast. I'm not sure what Heritage House is going to do once they try to bring the other rid-ing horses in.''

Ian shook his head at her question as he shooed the horse away. "Oh, he'll be fine. Just remind them to keep him with the mares. He likes the company better, and they don't hold his being a gelding against him."

Quinn watched as the great horse wheeled around on his back legs and thundered at a run across the meadow. "Makes you wonder what he was like before they nipped and tucked."

Ian shook his head, his gaze still after his old mount. "Broke three of my bones. I never knew getting on who was going to win, him or me. It was always a challenge."

A steeplechase jockey. Quinn had heard about the breed, the gentleman amateur who so loved the sport that he starved himself to meet weight restrictions, found work that would give him time off, risked injury and even death to fly over those hurdles at thirty miles an hour. An obsession, some said. A passion, those in the sport defended. Owners dropped for-tunes on nonwinning horses, the public queued up to watch a minute of heart-stopping action. Riders battled elements and luck and a ton of muscle and speed to be the first one over the hurdle. And in the blink of an eye, it was over.

"How long did you race?" Quinn asked as the two of them stood side by side watching Blackie frolic in the spring sun like a colt.

Ian looked over at her for a second. Maybe assessing her interest, maybe remembering. "Twelve years."

"They let you compete while you were in the service?"

"When I could."

Quinn stole her own look at him and saw that the pain was once again hidden away, safely inside where no one would see it. She was amazed at his control. "The Greens, you said."

Ian glanced at her again, then straightened away from the fence. "That's right."

She nodded, wondering how to ask, wondering whether she had the right anymore. She'd learned more in the past few minutes than she could from any interrogation. Even so, there were still things about Ian Matthews that intrigued her. In-consistencies that taunted as much as they annoyed.

"They taught you that trick with the trip wire?"

This time Ian tilted his head. "They did."

She nodded, eyes back on Blackie, her heart thudding a little. "How long have you been out of the service?"

For a moment the only sounds were the susurrous music of a breeze through the trees, the harsh laughter of jackdaws, the cry of gulls sailing far beyond the hills. Quinn didn't have the courage to face Ian with her suspicions, so she watched Blackie.

"Ah," Ian finally acknowledged, "you're wondering why I was so sensitive to something so very small."

Quinn eased her gaze his way to stumble over that small knowing smile of his. "Your reflexes are just a bit...acute for a businessman," she objected lamely. "That's all."

"There's a good reason for that." It wasn't until Quinn was facing him again that he finished, the expression on his face at once patient and amused. "One of those little beauties was the reason I have such a delicate step on the dance floor today," he told her. "It was in the Falklands. I suppose it's something that simply stayed closer to me than I imagined."

Quinn blushed to the roots of her hair, furious with herself. "I'm sorry. I, um, I didn't..."

Her gaze was fixed on the gravel at her feet. Before she knew what was happening, Ian reached out and cupped her chin in his hand, raising it until she had to face him.

His eyes were serious now, soft and friendly and understanding. "Nothing to be sorry for," he told her. "You weren't the one who laid the thing, were you?"

Quinn thought that she should have seen some kind of judgment in that expression, at least a modicum of reproach. After all, she'd interloped in a place in Ian's life that couldn't have been easy for him to share. And worse, she wanted more. She wanted to learn how it had happened, what it had meant to him, even beyond the loss of racing. She wanted somehow to make it better. And she had no business wanting that.

"Yes," he answered, almost as if he'd heard her, his fingers still beneath her chin, his eyes still sparkling with understanding. "It's part of the permanent package now. No, it doesn't usually bother me as much as it has recently. I've just been in to have the thing fine-tuned, and since your ghost friend has decided that I'm the bag of the week, she's made it a point to land me on that side each time."

"I'll talk to her," Quinn promised.

Ian's smile was devastating. "Not on my account." His thumb circled Quinn's jaw, the rasp as deliciously intimate as the glint in his eyes. "I rather like that matchmaking part."

Quinn stiffened, pulled away. "You do not. And don't encourage her."

He was still smiling, his hand out, his hair gleaming golden in the sunlight. "Why not? I think she has marvelous taste."

Her heart shouldn't have been skidding around behind her ribs like that. She shouldn't have been short of breath, as if she'd run up a very long hill. Quinn didn't lose control. Not anymore. And she faced a dire threat of losing it right now, to this man with his callused, warm hands and crystal-bright eyes.

"I think the two of us should do our best to avoid any more entanglements with her so we can get this house open in time for the first weekend." Quinn hadn't even realized she'd backed away. She lifted an accusatory hand. "Which reminds me. Lady Allison from the Berkeley Square office wants you to call her. It seems you're trodding her turf without proper permission. Not to mention the fact that you seem to have got hold of privileged information somehow, which is going to upset the crowd in reservations."

"What information?" he asked, dropping his hand. Did Quinn imagine that his face seemed to drain? He looked suddenly stark.

"About the first guests. Allison was asking about security, too. I think you'd better explain it to her before you and I sit down to the books this afternoon."

"On one condition," Ian bargained, casually taking hold of the fence again. Still too pale looking by half. "Promise you won't say anything to the colonel about the leg."

Quinn was all set to turn back to the house. Ian's earnest words brought her to a halt. "Whyever not?"

Ian's smile was wry. He lifted a hand in dismissal. "I'm not a person who really enjoys swapping tales of battle. I hope you understand."

Quinn was going to nod or murmur something polite. After all, she had no concept of what war could do to a person. She wasn't going to presume that Ian's request was out of hand. Suddenly, though, it became superfluous. She'd been correct. Ian had looked pale. The minute his words were out, his knees buckled.

"Ian!"

He waved her away, on his knees now, his head down, his arm wrapped around a post to keep him from ending up on his face. "Bloody anesthetic," he growled between slow, deep breaths. "It's why I hate hospitals. Takes forever to get the stuff out of my system."

Quinn was on her knees next to him before she realized it. His forehead was clammy, his eyes shut, his hand cold.

"What can I do?" she demanded.

He shook his head irritably. "Just give me a second. It'll pass."

It did. Within five minutes he was walking at her side back toward the house arguing the merits of English versus Western saddles. Even so, until she was sure he was back in his room to lie down for a minute, Quinn didn't quite breathe. He'd scared the hell out of her back there. Her heart didn't slow appreciably until she heard him stretch out on his bed, and she was down in the kitchen sipping lukewarm tea. Even then, the cup rattled a little.

It shouldn't have mattered so much.

It did.

"So far, the most likely place to get a good toehold is that priest hole behind the earl's bedchamber," Ian instructed into the phone as he lay flat on his back, a hand over his aching eyes. "It wouldn't be any kind of trick at all to get into the chapel without the household knowing. As far as I know, there aren't any other secret accesses. The security system is basic wiring, no pressure sensors or ultraviolet. It can be breached at the fuse box. Phone wires attach to the southeast corner of the building. The guest suites are all on the second floor, east and west wing. Stables around to the west that can provide cover."

"And the plans?" Leila asked in her impatient voice.

"Well, if I had a fax machine here, I'd send them to you, wouldn't I, love?" he asked just as irritably. His head was aching worse than when he'd got out of the hospital. His joints ached. Damn this stuff. It was getting worse every time. He knew he'd bloody well scared the wits out of Quinn. It had ended up providing a much-needed distraction. Nonetheless, next time they suggested he spend a day or two trying something new to stabilize his hip, he'll politely tell them where they could insert their instruments.

"And while we're on the subject," he added, his eyes closed, fingers rubbing at the ache. "If you don't get on the ball a bit better, we won't have any plans at all. Lady Allison Lansford is most upset that I've shown up here. I thought you were going to take care of all that."

"I did," Leila insisted blackly. "Just like you said. I can't help it if you can't get things straight."

Dear Leila. Ian spent a good few moments doing some serious fantasizing about the thin-lipped, military-precise woman and any number of instruments of torture in which he'd been trained.

"The plans," she snapped. "When?"

"Two days," he promised. "I'll be getting in to do some recon in the village in the next few days."

"Fine. Just see that you do."

Click.

"And a fine evening to you, too, Leila dear," he snarled as he dropped the receiver back in its cradle.

Time to get up and get some aspirin. Not to mention scouting the still-gleaming kitchen and laundry for any unexpected access areas. And then he had to sit down with Quinn for at least an hour and not give in to the temptation to bury his face in her hair and just hold on.

Nobody had predicted this one. He was supposed to come in, get back the information on the current layout of Hartley Hall, not to mention the best way to break in and take control of a building full of delegates, royalty and Royalty Protection Department people. And instead, he was trying to figure out how he could make the most of his time with a bewitching American gypsy. He was thinking about ghosts and matchmaking.

How did the old biddy know, after all? How had she waited three hundred years to torment him with that particular song? He'd been braced for laughter, for chains and squeals and any other unearthly thing she could throw at him, because he had no real concern one way or another about ghosts.

And then, deep in the night, as the old grandfather clock in the entryway struck one, its soft bangs rolling through the house, he'd heard it. Lilting, low, almost intimate. "Greensleeves." Foolishly, it was the one song that could still make him ache with loneliness. The lullaby his grandmother had claimed as her own, because it had been the song her late husband had courted her with all those years ago.

Foolish, useless romanticism. Idealism taught at the knee of an old woman who was the least idealistic person he'd ever known. And now, because of it, he was more restless than ever. He was imagining what it would be like if he were really Ian Matthews and all he had to worry about was buying some pile of medieval stones out in the bogs.

He'd get up now. He'd get on downstairs and pore over the drawings and see if he could find any other accesses. And then he'd sit down with Quinn, just the way he'd promised her.

In a minute.

When he felt a little more social.

Ian didn't see Quinn peek in an hour later. Nor did he feel her settle an afghan over him as he slept. But he dreamed his grandfather was singing to his grandmother.

Five

Gwynnup Green was a village of fishermen. Poured into the folds of earth that slid precipitously toward the sea, the Green, as the locals called it, consisted of a tumble of whitewashed houses that crowded the narrow winding lanes all the way down to the quay where the fishing boats lolled in the sand like fat fish left behind by a receding tide. Cars were forbidden on the streets, and the tourists who chose this little out-of-the-way spot over the more famous coastal towns like Polperro and St. Ives stayed in bed-and-breakfast hotels that supported themselves in the winter on pilchard. There were four pubs in town, and the colonel had taken Ian to every one.

Correction, Ian thought, snatching a glance over the rim of his pint to see Quinn in avid discourse with one of the local women. The colonel and Quinn had taken him. Quinn had said it was so that she could make sure Ian was all right. Ian suspected that what she was really doing was tweaking the colonel's nose, especially since he considered the pub nearly as sacrosanct as the London club.

The Three Horseshoes was a classic pub, noisy and smoky and dark. There was quite a crowd in for a Tuesday evening, and a dart match was going on in the back room. Most of the talk revolved around the day's catch and the state of the local fleet. Age-old concerns, precarious lives. Simple people who measured their lives in seasons.

Ian liked it here. He liked the people of the Green, hardy, unpretentious people who hadn't forgotten what honest work and loyalty meant. People who could be counted on to help if necessary without ever thinking to ask for recompense.

Which could be a problem to someone trying to pull off any kind of terrorist activity in their midst.

Quinn was halfway through the introduction before Ian even heard her. '' . . . from the acquisitions department of Heritage House,'' she was saying, one hand on Ian's sleeve and her head nodding between him and her conversation partner. ''He was the one who bought Hartley Hall.''

A mousy thing with dishwater hair and a lapful of knitting, the object of the introduction squinted. Then she frowned, ''No, he wasn't,'' she disagreed.

''No, I wasn't,'' Ian immediately concurred.

Quinn looked at him for verification.

He shrugged. ''I was doing a bout with the orthopedists when this all came up,'' he explained. ''Had another team in on it.'' Then, before more could be said on the matter—such as, for instance, who that team had been—he turned to Quinn's friend and smiled. ''I'm afraid I was daydreaming and didn't catch your name. Forgive me.''

The Matthews charm rarely failed when he thought to use it. It didn't then, either. Smiling like Princess Diana at a photo shoot, the woman shrugged away his bad manners.

''Bodrugan,'' she murmured, her blue eyes sparkling with intelligence. ''Morwena Bodrugan. My Peter's the man behind the bar, there. Pleasure to meet you, Mr. Matthews. The company's done a fair sweet job o' redoin' the hall.''

''Most of that credit goes to Miss Rutledge,'' Ian offered with a smile. ''Don't you think?''

''Oh, aye. And her havin' to deal with the lady, too.''

Quinn's chuckle was musical. ''Ian is well acquainted with Mary. He introduced himself at the house by falling into one of her traps.''

Morwena gave her head a knowing shake. ''She is a plague sometimes, that one.''

''You've seen her?'' Ian asked.

Morwena's nod was matter-of-fact. "Found my Peter for me, didn't she? Me mum and da didn't even let him in the house until we got her approval."

"Oh, you used her matchmaking services?" Ian asked, an eye on Quinn's frown. It was obvious she was waiting for him to bring up their own suspicions in that area. "Is she usually right?"

This time Morwena gave a quick flash of the fingers, protection against the evil eye—just in case. "It's got to the point hereabouts that nobody goes to the altar without first consultin' her."

"I imagine she enjoys that."

"Laughs all the time."

"What about now?" he asked Quinn. "We can't exactly have young lovers trooping in on paying guests in the middle of the night."

Quinn took a long sip from her gin-and-tonic and carefully set it back exactly on the ring the glass had left on the napkin before answering. "We worked something out with the townfolk," she admitted almost sheepishly. "If somebody needs to use the room, we're going to try to not book it during one of the nights of the full moon. If that's not possible, Morwena's sister owns one of the local restaurants. Very romantic and full of local color. She's offering a free candlelit dinner for two."

Ian couldn't help grinning. "That will take just enough time to get the prospective couples in and out. Although I imagine it's going to be difficult having to explain the bodies flying into the front pond if Mary expresses her displeasure."

"We'll work it out."

She still wasn't quite facing him. It made Ian want to laugh. "I also have the distinct feeling that the corporate offices don't know anything about this."

That brought her eyes up, and for the first time Ian saw pleading in them. It softened that deep brown until it looked almost as liquid as it had that afternoon when she'd been on her knees in front of him. A sweet, soulful brown that made a man think of madonnas and courtesans. He found he could easily get used to looking into that brown.

"Alistair came up with the idea," she admitted. "After all, he was born not more than fifteen miles away. He knows better than corporate what Mary means to the Green—"

"Which is why you asked him to manage the hotel," Ian agreed. "A policy of which I highly approve."

She was sliding her long fingers up and down her glass, smearing the condensation, mesmerizing Ian. "I can't think there's any harm in it."

"Are the guests going to know?"

She stiffened, as if he'd asked whether the public had just been invited to watch the Queen bathe. "Absolutely not. This isn't a tourist game to the people here."

Long fingers, sensitive fingers, glistening with damp. Ian found his eyes constantly straying to them, thinking what they'd feel like against his skin. He turned to Morwena. "She's always right, you say?"

"Wouldn't hurt a few of the royal family to consult her."

Ian knew that neither woman would understand his smile. "It occurs to me," he observed, looking down into his own severely depleted glass before shooting Quinn a telling glance, "that we have yet to spend any time together in the good lady's chambers."

He'd been expecting it. He'd hoped for it, that small tell-tale flush at the base of her throat. Her emotional barometer. His smile broadened.

"It's hip deep in paint buckets and wallpaper rolls right now," she said defensively, intent on her actions.

Ian nodded and turned to Morwena Bodrugan. "Sir Alistair is of the opinion that Mary means to match Miss Rutledge and myself."

Morwena's eyes grew wide. "Is he?"

Quinn's throat darkened.

Ian nodded with absolute sincerity. "It seems that the countess has been conspiring to throw us together in the oddest places. I guess maybe we'd better be the next ones to make use of a full moon, do you think?"

"Oh, for God's sake..." Quinn blurted.

But Morwena was giving Ian the once-over. "Only five days away, if that's what you're thinkin'. 'Course, nobody's really lived with her in so long, maybe she's just decided not to wait till then."

Ian smiled and nodded, but his mind was quickly interpreting the woman's new posture. More rigid, more certain, as if she'd just been given some kind of say in his life. Which, to her way of thinking, she had.

Ian could tell that all the Green considered Quinn one of
their own, a rather eccentric American cousin, as it were. The
foreigner who guarded their ways more fiercely than their own
countrymen in London did. It left Ian with the feeling that he
would be called to account by a very unamused populace if he
ever hurt Quinn.

For the first time since he'd hobbled up to that great gray
pile of stone, Ian wondered if he didn't have more to worry
about from these folk than from a rather ruthless ghost.

He realized, just by looking at the telling expression in
Morwena Bodrugan's eyes, that Quinn and the colonel had
succeeded in what they'd set out to do—make Hartley Hall
even a more cherished and integral part of the community of
Gwynnup Green. Probably more than any time since Mary had
organized the locals into a food cooperative, the citizens considered the hall theirs, and theirs to defend. No outsider would
get their help in taking it.

So then there would probably be no assault from the sea if
the locals were kept informed. It would have to be by moor.
And that, if Ian's tribulations over those Cornish roads meant
anything, would be a difficult thing to do.

"Last round!" Morwena's husband suddenly called from
his place at the taps. Morwena looked up a bit guiltily, obviously having neglected her duties to sit with her new friend.

"Please," Quinn suddenly said, a hand waylaying the
woman. "Don't say anything. Not even to Peter."

Morwena was obviously dumbstruck. "But why not?" she
demanded. "It's cause for celebration in these parts."

"At least give us until the full moon," Ian suggested,
shamelessly glad to see the gratitude in Quinn's eyes. "That
way if I find myself sharing room with the carp, I won't be
quite so disgraced."

Morwena smiled and patted Quinn's hand as if Quinn were
a callow child, when in fact Morwena couldn't have had five
years on her. "Don't you worry, love. There's just some things
the menfolk don't need to know quite yet, now, aren't there?"

"I say, old man," the colonel boomed as Morwena disappeared back into the crowd. "Another round before we tod-
dle off?"

Ian lifted his glass with a rueful shake of his head. "Bloody
quacks have limited my intake, don't ya know."

Alistair's laugh would have called ships to the shoals. "But we haven't toasted the regiment yet!"

Not at the Three Horseshoes, at any rate. There they'd only made it through the various members of the royal family and, in deference to Quinn, the "colonies." They'd taken good care of the regiment at the Royal George, the Silver Spurs and the Cock 'n' Bull. Ian's head was throbbing again, and he wanted to get to bed. That was if the old witch would let him sleep tonight.

"I hope you don't mind, Sir Alistair," Quinn piped up, looking suddenly very tired, "but it's been a long day. How 'bout if Ian walks me home, and you can follow?"

"No, no, you great sod, Patton did not beat Monty there!" the colonel bellowed to one of his tablemates, evidently in answer to an opinion. "Politics, man, don't you know anything? Yes, yes, quite, my dear. See that you take care, and don't lock the door."

Another great bawling laugh and a crippling slap on the back to his table partner sent him back into the fray of the Italian campaign.

"You're looking tired," Quinn said to Ian as she preceded him out into the night.

After the close quarters in the Horseshoes, the darkness seemed infinite. Ian took a second to lift his head and take a few great drafts of salt air before answering. The sky was vast, with the diamond dusting of stars playing hide-and-seek among scudding clouds. The constant throb of the ocean could be heard right up High Street, and the lights of the town dissolved into spills of milk with the first tendrils of fog that snaked up the valley. A beautiful, sleepy, untouched place. Even though it looked little like it, the Green reminded him of the Yorkshire moors, and he missed them.

"Oh, I wouldn't say tired so much," Ian admitted, turning to take hold of Quinn's arm as they headed out of town. "Bested. I keep forgetting just what that blasted anesthetic does to me until it's too late. I'm afraid my stamina isn't what it should be."

She looked up at him, and he could only imagine the concern in those luminous eyes of hers. All he could see in the dark that descended on them as they stepped away from the lights of the Horseshoes was the milky impression of skin, the smoky tumble of hair. Above the salt and the fog, he could smell a garden, and knew it was hers.

"You should have said something sooner," she accused.

He smiled into the darkness. "I was enjoying watching you too much."

That didn't seem to sit well. Ian felt her stiffen in his grasp and turn to face the consuming darkness.

"So, what are you going to do?" she asked, her voice soft and uncertain.

Ian had been so busy enjoying her proximity, the gentle scent of her on the night, that he almost didn't hear her.

"About what?" he asked, glancing at her. And then regretting it. She had on a sweater and skirt, regulation uniform for a woman in England. Somehow, though, even with the chilly night air, she'd managed to pick something soft and flowing, so that it belled out from her like an undulating wave and outlined the shape of her legs. Her very long legs. Her very nice legs.

She was looking down, not even aware that Ian was suddenly thinking very ungentlemanly thoughts. "About telling corporate of our, um, unusual agreement with the Green." Lifting her head, she looked up at him, her forehead creased, her voice betraying what the people here meant to her.

Ian suddenly couldn't manage to think and walk at the same time. Neither, it seemed, could Quinn. The two of them came to an uncertain halt in the middle of the lane, twenty feet beyond the edge of town, with the heartbeat of the ocean matching their own.

Ian took hold of her other arm, as well, turning her fully toward him. Needing to reassure her, to comfort her. Feeling the brush of that skirt against his legs, now, and thinking that she wasn't close enough.

"I think I can promise," he said, bending his head to her, "that Gwynnup Green will not hear a word from Heritage House about your special arrangement." He had no right saying that. He'd catch hell for it. It didn't matter. He could see her lips now, smiling, relieved. So soft and dark in the night, so promising.

"Especially," he said, knowing that was getting into far more trouble than he already was, bending to taste her lips, anyway, "if Mary's right."

She never got the chance to protest. Pulling her to him, Ian kissed her. Then he kissed her again. Kissed her long and hard, like he'd been wanting to do all along, with her legs pressed right against his, her belly against his groin, her breasts crushed against his chest until he ached to fold them into his palm.

He forced her head back and caught it in his hand, wrapping his fingers into her hair. She murmured, a little whisper of surprise, of dismay, that melted into pleasure as she brought her own hand up to his chest.

Ian tasted a touch of bitterness on her tongue. He sipped at it, a delicious contrast to the sweet smell of her skin, the soft, pliant feel of her body. He filled his hands with her, his mouth with her. He ached with a sudden yearning that swept away sense and logic and memory. In the darkness, at the edge of a town he'd never before seen, posing as a man he could never be, he burned for a woman he could never have. And for a very brief moment, he believed that it all didn't matter. That ghosts could tell the future and that his had just changed.

Ian pulled free just shy of the point of no return. His arms still pinning Quinn to him, he closed his eyes and rested his cheek against her hair.

"Are you going to pass out again?" she asked in a hesitant voice, her head against his chest.

"No," he managed, sounding pretty out of breath himself. "I'm going to behave like a gentleman and stop before I pull you right into the heather."

There was a moment of heartstopping silence. A small movement within his arms. An even smaller voice. "Oh."

"We should get on before someone runs us over right in the middle of the road, don't you think?"

Another silence, as if she really had to make up her mind. "I imagine."

Ian nodded, his head still resting atop hers, his arms still holding her up, her arms doing much the same.

And then, without another word, the two stepped apart and walked on to the hall.

"Greensleeves" again. Quinn sorely wished Mad Mary would get another title on her hit parade. For some reason, that one was beginning to get to her. Soft, melodic, romantic.

Sad. Maybe Mary would take to a suggestion to try something more appropriate, like "Another Saturday Night, and I Ain't Got Nobody."

All Quinn would have to do was suggest it, and she'd be on her own keester in the fish pond.

Surely it was the lack of sleep that was wrecking her concentration today. She'd already lost the floor plans to the west wing and told the paperhangers to hang the paper upside down. Twice. She hadn't had the nerve to do any of her own work for fear she'd ruin something irretrievable.

Or she could blame it on Ian. Every time she sat down for more than five minutes, she kept reliving those moments on the road the night before. She still ached in the funniest place, a place that hadn't ached since she'd fallen head over heels for Jason Aubuchon, Right Person, Preppy Personified.

That ache should have been warning enough. Should have been her warning bell that all logic systems were about to break down. Instead, it had the curious effect of making her want to smile. And hum. And damn if she didn't keep finding herself humming "Greensleeves." It got to the point by lunchtime that Alistair was shooting her very arch looks and the workmen were whispering.

She should have been a lot more worried. Instead, she couldn't stop grinning.

"Have you seen Ian?" she asked Alistair.

Pulling off his reading glasses, the old man looked up from the local history book he was consulting on behalf of the tiny wizened woman who sat across from him.

"Oh, excuse me," Quinn apologized, stepping farther into the room. "I didn't see you, Mrs. Bumphries. How are you today?"

The little woman nodded, much like a duchess viewing one of the gamekeepers. "Very well, thank you, my dear. Sir Alistair is helping me in local research for the foundation. To prove that the white-rumped titmouse is indigenous to the area and therefore worthy of consideration for preservation. We are so hoping to construct viaducts for the little fellows beneath the motorways."

Mrs. Bumphries had already accomplished the construction of viaducts for migrating toads so that traffic didn't impede their mating rituals. When the little woman and her band got started, all Quinn could do was smile noncommittally. Which was what she did now.

"You really should join the Gentle Friends of Small Creatures in Albion," she said brightly, as she did every time Quinn saw her. And, just like every other time, Quinn wanted to ask why the group couldn't have come up with a name for their organization that had a catchy acronym. All you got from the Gentle Friends was GFSCA. They could have tried something like FURRIE, Friends of Underprivileged Rodents and Raccoons in England.

"Such a worthy cause," Mrs. Bumphries said.

"Yes, I know," Quinn conceded with a straight face. "I've seen the red sweaters you've knitted for the squirrels. Any luck getting them on?"

The wizened face fell a little. "Not quite yet. We're most hopeful, though. We did have a splendid turnout for the roadblock we set up to preserve the ancient oak and its lovely nest of sparrows, however. Kept the road crew waiting most of a morning. Quite brilliant, all in all. Amaryllis Fellinworth served cucumber sandwiches. You must join us next time."

"If I can," Quinn promised with another vague smile, then turned back to Alistair. "Ian?" she asked.

"Last I saw of him, he was making up to that great beast down by the stables," Alistair announced, fingering his glasses. "Have you seen it? Blackie's more docile than a dog around the man. Absolutely extraordinary, ya ask me."

"Isn't it?" Quinn agreed, wondering whether Ian's relationship with the horse was up for general conversation. She decided to leave it alone for now. "He had an appointment to meet with some of the craftspeople now."

Alistair was already putting his glasses back on. "Probably up in his room. Said something about being red-faced that a Hussar could outdrink a Green Jacket." His smile was directed at the book, and at his own pride. "The service just ain't what it used to be."

Quinn figured that was about all she was going to get, so she turned back toward the stairs and Ian's room. All about her, the hall rang with the echoes of workmen. Carpet was being laid in the Gainsborough salon, and the kitchen appliances were being outfitted. The final stonework was being fitted for the fireplace in the old great hall, and the wine steward was stocking the cellar.

It wouldn't be long now. Hartley Hall would open, there would be new jobs in the Green, guests would enjoy the meticulously assembled ambiance of the house, and Quinn would be off to London to work with Allison on the proposals for Stratham Castle in Scotland.

The sound of her footsteps as she mounted the staircase joining the clamor, Quinn took her usual look up the length of the stairs. She savored the rich wood, the nascent light that streamed in through the leaded windows, the audience of dour Elizabethan faces that greeted her.

She was going to miss them all. Mary and Alistair and Morwena and the special feeling of home that pervaded the hall. She'd wandered the world almost continuously since her eighteenth birthday and never once felt the need to slow down, the next place always more exciting than the last. But since being here, since seeing the special warmth in Ian's eyes, she'd begun to wonder.

Her contribution to society had always been her careful, loving restorations, so that the wonders of another era wouldn't die. Quinn, who had no sense of personal time, recreated someone else's. Cared for it, crafted it, resurrected it for everyone to appreciate. An adopted child enjoying lineage vicariously through others. But maybe soon she'd consider her own time. Starting with her and going forward instead of back.

Maybe soon.

"Ian?" The heavy wood absorbed the sound of her knock. Down the hall the painters were clattering about in the Edwardian bedroom. When they were finished, they were going to retouch the trim in the hallway. At their own expense.

She thought she heard a murmur. Knocking again, she called louder. "Ian? It's one o'clock. We need to see the craftspeople."

This time, Quinn was certain she heard a groan. If she'd knocked first thing in the morning after hearing what the colonel had said, she would have laughed the sound off and walked away. But she'd seen Ian at breakfast, a bit pale and quiet, which she'd put down to the fact that neither of them had talked all the rest of the way home, and had done little more than offer mutual good-nights upon retiring.

But in the middle of the day? Quinn didn't have a qualm about pushing the door open.

"Oh, dear God..."

She was across the room before she even realized it.

"Damn...shouldn't be...happening..." Ian mumbled. He was in bed, tangled in the sheets, curled in fetal position, pale as death and shaking so hard the bed was trembling. His teeth chattered so loudly she could hear the sound all the way across the room.

His eyes were open, but he was having trouble focusing. His arms were wrapped tightly around himself for warmth, his body racked by vicious tremors that wouldn't stop.

"What is it?" she demanded, frantic. Quinn wasn't any good at medical things. She'd once passed out when her father had cut himself slicing a watermelon. Her knowledge of treatment didn't go beyond starving a cold and feeding a fever. Or was it the other way around?

Reaching out, she laid a hesitant hand on Ian's forehead, not even sure what she should feel. Certain that she shouldn't feel skin that was quite so deathly cold.

"Sorry..." he chattered, convulsed again. "It's a... bother..."

"Oh, God," she moaned, truly frightened. His features were taut, his hands in spasm. "What do I do? What's wrong?"

But he couldn't seem to answer.

Whirling on her heel, Quinn raced to the door. "Alistair!" she shrieked, desperate, torn between running for help and leaving Ian alone.

Down the hall, a bucket clanged and a workman popped his head out the door.

"Problems, love?"

"Get the colonel!" she yelled at him. "Mr. Matthews is ill!"

She waited just long enough to see the man comply before turning back to the room. Terror bubbled in her throat, dreadful hesitation.

There were extra blankets in the chest. She'd get them. She'd warm Ian up. Maybe that would help. She'd no more than yanked a couple out and made it to the side of the bed before Alistair blew through the door.

"Get away from that man!" he shouted.

Startled, Quinn dropped the blankets on the floor. She took a quick look at Ian, another at Alistair. "Why? What's wrong?"

Alistair bristled, his hand thrown out in agitation. "Why, he's naked, of course."

He was. Quinn simply hadn't taken the time to notice.

"Alistair, for God's sake, get in here and help," she snapped, bending to sweep up the blankets. "Something's really wrong."

"Young miss—"

Quinn leveled one killing glare on him, and he surrendered. But his mustache trembled with indignation.

"Please, Alistair," she begged. "He's so sick."

"'Course he is," he agreed heartily, striding in. "Hong Kong?" he asked Ian as he helped Quinn spread blankets. "Indonesia?"

Ian's smile looked more like rictus. "Zimbabwe."

"Ah," Alistair nodded sagely. "Quite. How long ago?"

"Last . . . year. . . . They swore I was through . . . with it . . ."

"Bloody quacks. Never do get it right, do they?"

"Alistair!" Quinn said shrilly, her patience vanished.

Alistair smiled. "Simple, really. A close encounter with an *anopheles*, which infects the human host with the horrid little beasts. This would be *Plasmodium vivax,* of course, since it's recurrent. *Plasmodium falciparum* is always worse, but it's a single course. Extraordin'ry, really. The chills occur when the little merozites escape from the ruptured erythrocyte. The ensuing fever, of course, is the reaction to all that debris floating around unattended in the system. Bloody bother."

"What," Quinn demanded, since Ian seemed too incapacitated to speak, "are you talking about?"

Alistair turned to her as if she were a very slow child who asked silly questions. "Why, malaria, of course."

Six

"**M**alaria?" Quinn squeaked, now even more upset.

Ian didn't look particularly surprised. Of course, his eyes were squeezed shut as he shook, the new layer of blankets pulled tight around his neck.

"Quite," Alistair agreed with a brisk nod. "Tertian, most commonly. Forty-eight-hour cycle. Chills, fever, sweat. Then all over again. His temperature will probably top out at 106 degrees or so by nightfall."

Quinn realized she was wringing her hands. "A hundred and six?" Visions of convulsions and death tormented her.

"Oh, quite. At least. I've seen cases where it's hit 108. Fried the devil like a kipper, don't ya know."

"What do we do?" she demanded, certainly not needing the rather graphic discourse. Her imagination was providing quite vivid enough pictures. "Should I call a doctor?"

Alistair waved off the notion. "Nonsense. We can handle it here without much fuss, can't we, lad?"

He was in full regimental mode now, Quinn could see. Pretty soon he'd demand that Ian buck up and think of queen and country. Much to her surprise, though, Ian readily agreed.

"No . . . hospital," he grated between chattering teeth.

"But Ian—"

"No!"

"You have some chloroquine, I take it?" Alistair asked.

Quinn thought she saw a nod.

Leaning over to dispense a restorative punch on the shoulder, Alistair let off a booming laugh. "Shouldn't have wasted your time on ale last night, old man. Should have had gin and tonic. Would have had your quinine quite painlessly, what? You can swallow, of course."

"Yes."

Another brisk nod. "Good chap."

Quinn looked around. "That's it?"

"'Course not," he bellowed. "He'll need antipyretics. And lashings of water. You'll get that for me, there's a girl."

"Once I know what's going on," she grated.

Alistair was already heading toward the bathroom. "Toilet kit?"

Ian didn't quite answer. Quinn walked up to the side of the bed. Malaria. God, all she knew about it was what she'd seen in old war movies. Shaking, sweating, jaundiced men who wasted away. Brutal chills, high fevers. Her only experience with high fevers had been when she'd had pneumonia some years ago in Italy. Her temperature had soared so high they'd packed her in ice. Not one of her more pleasant memories. Neither were the fever-induced nightmares. She wasn't at all sure she was the person to help Ian through this.

The problem was that suddenly she couldn't be anywhere else.

Reluctantly she followed Alistair in to where he was rifling through Ian's leather bag. He'd already dumped most of the contents out into the sink, and nothing looked particularly out of the ordinary.

"His chills don't look any better," she protested. "Isn't there something else we can do?"

Alistair's attention was on his cache. "Body heat, of course," he suggested, still digging through toothpaste and sewing kits. "Worked wonders in Burma when old Piggy Fogbellows came down with it. Daughter of a local chieftain offered her services. *And* her brother's. Odd lot, that. They spent five days squeezing old Piggy in like a ham sandwich." His laugh ricocheted around the tiled walls.

Quinn took a quick look over her shoulder. Ian was naked under there. Naked and unforgettable, with a physique she'd never anticipated on an Englishman, whom she'd always considered just a little pale and thin for her taste. He was hard and lean and well muscled, and just the thought of crawling under the covers with him produced another type of chill altogether.

"Do you think you could do that?" she asked instead, shoving suddenly damp hands into her work-pants pockets.

Alistair dropped the can of shaving cream to the floor with a clang. "My dear girl," he objected angrily, whirling on her, "I was in the army. Not the navy."

Quinn ducked her head in concession. "Then I'll do it."

Another article hit the floor. "Absolutely not. That man is quite undressed."

Quinn glared at him. "Then what do you suggest we do?"

His head was going to explode. His joints shrieked in agony. He was on fire, he was freezing. Ian tried to push the great mass of covers off him without success. It seemed he had no strength, either. He was suffocating. The world shuddered more closely into focus, a cold, agonizing place outside the furnace that was his body.

He knew what was wrong. He'd fought this before. The fever was beginning to soar, where his body would collapse and his mind would swim. He'd hallucinate and fight and beg for relief, and not remember any of it. And then, if the colonel didn't find his chloroquine, it would start all over again.

The weight. He pushed against it again and realized that it was a body. Another person in his bed, curled right against him, the heat they threw off doubling and tripling his own.

"Here, Ian," a soft voice coaxed, as long fingers slipped into the damp hair at the back of his head. "Have something to drink."

Nothing. He wanted nothing. He wanted just to slide back into oblivion. He wanted that weight against him gone.

Just a minute. That voice. Quinn's voice, soft, concerned, frightened. Was it she? He vaguely remembered hearing her voice echoing around the bathroom, asking Alistair about how to ease the chills. Body heat.

Her body?

He was lying on his side. It always helped somehow, easing the fire in his hip. It was a struggle, but Ian managed to get his eyes open.

He'd been right. Someone was in bed with him. Someone heavy enough to push him to the other side. Mournful eyes examined him from not three inches away. A head came up to acknowledge his presence. And then a long pink tongue snaked out to lick his face.

"Bloody hell..."

"Oh, good." Quinn sighed in relief from the edge of the bed. "You're awake."

"Get this blasted...dog..."

"Come on, Copenhagen," she coaxed, and the bed sprang up empty. "That's a good boy. He kept you warm," she admonished Ian as she lifted his head, which felt like a leaden weight, and tipped a cup against his lips.

Cold water dribbled half into his mouth and half across his face. Ian didn't care. He needed to be cool right now.

"Aspirin," he croaked, shoving listlessly again at the blankets.

"Coming right up." She let his head down and dispatched with the blankets. Goose bumps erupted all across his back as the cool air found him through the sheets.

His stomach was heaving again. God, he hoped he could keep the chloroquine down. Had he taken it yet? He couldn't remember. He was drifting again, sliding into the mists, his body too dissipated to fight it.

He had to swallow that aspirin first, or he'd be swinging at Quinn like the quartermaster. Like Hans the night of the Munich raid.

"My...medicine?"

"Couldn't find it. Evidently you forgot it this trip. Alistair's off scaring up the village doc. Says he knows that between him and the chemist we can take good care of things."

Ian got the aspirin down. Barely. More water soaked his hair. His throat was parched and sore from the tablets sticking halfway down. When he coughed, Quinn sat right on the bed and propped him up against her chest. Ian closed his eyes, unaccustomed to such comfort. His chest ached in a new way, and he thought he'd have to fight tears soon.

Then, as she lay him back down and readjusted the sheets around him, she bent so that they were face-to-face.

"And when you get better," she suggested with a smile that was just a shade too controlled, "you can explain this."

And she pointed a gun right at him. His own gun. The .9mm Browning he'd hidden all the way at the back of his garment bag so no one could find it.

Ian gave up without a fight. He just sighed and closed his eyes and let the mists overtake him.

A gun. Quinn still couldn't believe that she'd found it while she and the colonel had been tearing through Ian's things looking for that damn bottle of pills. She'd scraped her knuckles against it, at the bottom of a garment bag in the wardrobe, a small, lethal-looking thing that had fit neatly into her palm. A thirteen-round 9 mm semiautomatic Browning pistol.

She knew because her father had collected guns. She'd never shared the enthusiasm, but she'd learned some of the information by osmosis. And she knew that this wasn't a gun that one used for a hunt—one must have a proper Purdy shotgun for that, the colonel always said. It certainly wasn't a legal gun. Not in England, anyway. The only people allowed guns in this country were the services and a select few of the special-police branches. And, as far as she knew, neither had expressed any interest in Hartley Hall.

So, who exactly was Ian Matthews, and what did he want here?

It had been an hour since she'd shown him the gun and demanded answers. An hour since he'd slipped back into unconsciousness. Quinn had yet to leave his bedside, pulling one of her own wing chairs close so she could force some liquids on him as he tossed and turned and muttered beneath the crumpled sheet. She'd bullied him into drinking some water, held him when he'd choked, wiped his burning forehead with a cloth. Bitten her nails to the quick. Waited with increasing desperation for the colonel to get back.

It terrified Quinn, because she didn't know what to do. The fever was soaring, baking Ian, shimmering off his body like sun from a Manhattan street. He was beginning to lash out. Twice he'd batted her hand away when she'd come close, and once he'd called her a few of the names he'd used on Mary. If she couldn't get more fluids down, would he convulse? If she needed to get more aspirin down him, would he tolerate it? Just how high could his temperature go before she had to worry? Worry more? Panic?

"No, Brian, don't.... Get back!"

Quinn sat upright in the chair. Ian was trying to get up, his eyes open but opaque, his face screwed up in fear.

"Ian, lie down," she coaxed. "It's all right."

She took hold of him by the shoulders, intending to ease him back in the bed. She only managed to trigger some kind of memory. Ian grabbed her arms and pulled her over. Right on top of him.

"Where is he?" he demanded in her ear.

She tried to wriggle free. His chest was burning her through her blouse. His cheek seared hers. Her heart thumped even harder than his. His grip, for a sick man, was like steel.

"Ian, please..."

His chest heaved with the exertion, but even so he held tight. "Damn it, I asked you a question."

His voice was so clear, so cold. Quinn wondered what he saw with those fierce gray eyes of his. He wasn't even watching her, but staring over her shoulder. But still he wouldn't let her go. And she couldn't pull herself free.

For some reason, this all amused Mary. The booming laugh echoed up and down the halls like the sound of a train in a tunnel.

"I...I don't know," Quinn tried desperately, not sure what he wanted to hear. "He was here just a minute ago."

"If you've done anything to him...you vicious bastard..."

"I promise. He was fine."

"He wasn't—" he shook her, hard "—fine. He was hurt. He needs my help." His voice fell, a deadly whisper that Quinn didn't recognize. "What do you think I'll do to her if you don't tell me?"

Her instinct was to struggle. Suddenly she didn't know this man. She thought of the nasty little gun and the unanswered questions, and it frightened her almost as much as the fever.

"I say, young lady, aren't you getting just a bit enthusiastic?"

Quinn whipped her head around to find Alistair at the door, red-faced and blustering like an outraged father.

"Make him let go," she begged, wishing she could just let her head drop alongside Ian's, just as he'd done so long ago...two days ago. Oh, God, this was becoming impossible.

Alistair walked right up to the bed and scared the hell out of Quinn.

"'Ten-shun!" he bawled right in Ian's ear.

Ian let go so fast Quinn almost rolled onto the floor. Then both she and Ian seemed to be in the process of pulling themselves up.

"At ease, lads," Alistair boomed.

Ian settled right back down. Quinn climbed off the bed, even more red-faced than the colonel.

"He was delirious," she defended herself. "I was afraid he was going to hurt himself."

Alistair did his own version of the eyebrow opinion. "Quite."

Her hands shaking, Quinn pushed her hair out of her eyes and straightened to face him. "Did you get the medicine?"

That seemed to galvanize the old man. "Naturally. Now, it's just a matter of getting it down. Did you manage with the aspirin?"

"Yes." Quinn took another look to where Ian lay, the sheet tangled around his waist, the water she'd been cooling him with glistening on his chest. "But I don't think it's made much difference. He's so hot."

She'd seen his hip, too, the ugly puckering of skin that had marked the original injury, the neat tracks of successive surgeries radiating from it. It had been massive, traumatic. She was amazed at how much it hurt her to see it. She wanted to touch it, to soothe the agony that scarring must have caused.

But what, she thought, looking back at his taut, anxious face as he mumbled and plucked at his linen, had really caused the injury? Had it been the Falklands, as he'd said? Had he really been in the service, or was it all a fabrication?

For some reason Quinn hadn't shown the colonel the gun. She wanted to hear what Ian had to say first. She still, even now, wanted to trust him.

First, though, she had to make sure he didn't die.

Then she'd grill him so hard he'd wish he had.

"Right, then," the colonel announced, making a production of pulling out the packet of pills. "A gram now, 500 milligrams at six, twenty-four and forty-eight hours." He reached out to test Ian's forehead himself and came away frowning. "You're quite correct, though. He's burning up. I'd wager he'll top off at over 106 easily. And, of course, if we don't get the chloroquine in him, this will all happen again in two days. If we're lucky, of course."

Quinn sorely wished he wouldn't sound quite so jolly about it.

"How can we tell?" she demanded. "He can't hold a thermometer in his mouth."

Alistair blustered again. "Only one decent way to get a temperature. You haven't done it yet?"

"Oh, no, you don't," she argued, arms instinctively across her chest. "That's where *I* draw the line."

Alistair actually smiled. "I suppose we could try it beneath the arm. Add a degree, what."

In the end, they came up with 104.8. And it had been rising only an hour.

"How do we get it down?" Quinn demanded, her eyes on Ian.

The consideration of that question seemed to involve quite a few facial muscles and most of the colonel's hair. Quinn had never seen so much movement above his neck before.

"Could use alcohol baths," he finally said. "But I'm deuced if I know how to get him as far as the tub."

"What about packing him in ice?" Quinn asked.

Alistair bristled mightily. "My dear girl, that's a three-hundred-year-old bed! Do you know what water would do to it?"

Ian was moaning, his mouth open, his hands opening and closing against the sheets. Quinn was terrified. "We'll use a painting tarp. Certainly we can spare one or two. I imagine corporate wouldn't begrudge us saving one of its executives."

If, in fact, he *was* an executive. Sometime, when she thought of it, Quinn was going to have to call Lady Allison just to be sure.

"The freezers are in," she insisted. "We have the ice. We'll protect the bed. Come on, Alistair, let's not wait until he's having seizures."

"We'll need to restrain him," he suggested. "That ice hits him, he'll go wild." One long look at Quinn resurrected everything the colonel had seen upon walking into the room.

"And we know what he's capable of when he's delirious, don't we?"

He was in agony. Freezing, burning, buried in the snow. Was he at Hereford? Was it interrogation training? He couldn't remember. They'd tied him down, chest and waist and legs, leaving only his hands. But he couldn't move them. They were weighted, frostbitten. Maybe they'd left him in the Brecons, softening him up for the lights and action.

Well, he'd volunteered for it. Too damn smart by half, his father had always said. Couldn't follow in his brother's footsteps like a good lad.

It was dark. Night. Ian was shivering and wet, so it must have been raining. Sleeting, because he was still freezing. He thought his fingers would fall off.

It was all right, though. Billingsgate would find him. He'd make sure that nobody took him prisoner. That nobody would make him break.

It was a struggle, but Ian opened his eyes. They were gritty and swollen, as if he'd been crying. But that was absurd. An SAS officer doesn't cry. Not even if your partner dies by slow degrees in front of you.

He felt slow, confused. Blinking a few times, he tried to get his surroundings into focus.

It wasn't interrogation. They wouldn't have left the lights off for a second. Then where?

A fitful moon poured in the window alongside his bed. The room was a forest of shadows, massive beasts that crouched against the whitewashed walls that were nothing but ghosts in the night. Ian couldn't stop shaking. He couldn't collect his thoughts.

Then he saw the door, and it was closed. Closed, except that there was a woman standing in front of it. A silent, imperious-looking woman with laughing eyes, who wore the oddest attire.

A costume party? Maybe he'd been kidnapped by a group of party-goers who dressed up like Elizabeth I. Extraordinary. She was chuckling, as if Ian were the funniest thing she'd ever seen. And then, oddly, singing. "Greensleeves," sounding exactly like his grandmother. It made him want to cry again. Except, of course, that he didn't cry.

"Help me," he begged, except that it came out a listless croak.

She just smiled and sang and faded away.

And then Ian saw the other woman. Closer. Much prettier. Asleep in the chair by the bed, her legs curled up under her, hair tumbled, her face pale and weary. A pietà, he thought. A grieving madonna carved just for him. He would sing "Greensleeves" for her, and maybe she'd dance with him.

He tried to sing, but his voice was still a croak, his throat as parched as his eyes. As battered as his body, which must have sustained a lot of punishment.

He was so tired. He was about to give up and just sleep when the woman opened her eyes. The madonna, with eyes the color of fresh earth, with a smile that could break a man's heart.

"Ian?" she whispered, and he remembered.

"Cold," he managed. Struggled against his bonds until he realized that he didn't even have the strength to move. His body simply refused to comply. He was drenched, the sweat rolling into his eyes and melting the ice piled up under his arms and over his belly. Suddenly he was concerned that the legacy he'd inherited could be passed on to another generation. He couldn't quite feel anything there, either.

She climbed to her feet and eased onto the side of the bed, still wearing the work pants and cotton shirt she'd had on that morning. Or the morning before. When she rested her hand against his forehead, it felt like silk. Like sunlight. Then she smiled, and Ian weakened even more.

"You scared me," she accused softly, pushing his soaking hair back off his forehead with that soft, strong hand. "You've been yelling and tossing for hours. We finally had to tie you down."

"And...freeze my..."

He could only imagine the blush. He didn't imagine the flight her eyes took before she dipped her head with discomfort. "Well, you're sweating now. Alistair said that was the last stage. I think we can dispense with the ice."

"A...brilliant...idea," he approved as heartily as a strangled whisper allowed.

What he hadn't realized was that she was going to do it herself. If only he had more strength. Any strength. He watched her, as efficient as any nurse, and let his body be turned back and forth until the plastic beneath him was dispensed into the tub and clean sheets were in place. By which time he knew why men always fell in love with their nurses.

"Get some sleep now," she commanded, straightening the sheets over him.

"Did I get the chloroquine?" he asked.

She grinned. "Barely. The colonel had to scare some up in town, and by the time we got it into you, it was like trying to feed an unhappy tiger. You choked and gagged and called me names I think even embarrassed Alistair."

"Then I'm sorry."

"Don't be sorry yet," she advised. "When you wake up tomorrow, you and I are going to talk."

He grimaced. "I suppose my cover is blown."

"Like a farmhouse door in a tornado. I found your gun when we were hunting for chloroquine. The bits and pieces I heard while you were delirious made for interesting entertainment."

"The colonel . . . ?"

She peered at Ian, evidently coming to some kind of decision. " . . . will find out when I decide to tell him. So you get one shot at it. Now, get some sleep."

Ian grabbed hold of her hand before she had a chance to turn away. "Only if you will, too."

Again, he could imagine the blush. "I'll be asleep five minutes after you close your eyes," she promised.

Ian couldn't help stroking her palm with his thumb. A small movement, but an effort. He was so tired. So beaten and drained. But still he couldn't quite let her go. "Malaria isn't contagious, you know."

Quinn smiled. "Unless one of us happens to be a mosquito."

Ian made it a point to look down the length of his body. "I think I can vouch for myself."

"You don't have to."

He looked up to find something in her eyes he'd never seen before. Something dark and indecipherable. Something that made his old weary pulse quicken. When he pulled gently on her arm, she came to him.

"You sure you're up to this?" she whispered, hands against his chest.

He managed a chuckle. "After being packed in ice like that, I'm not certain I'll be up to anything ever again."

A bald lie. Even now he felt the first stirrings, at once irritating and reassuring. He wasn't dead yet. He just couldn't do anything about it.

He could, however, kiss her. And he did, marshaling all his strength to reach up and wrap his fingers into her hair, tasting the fresh air on her, the life in her. Replenishing his own energy with the sweet spark of her touch, her fingers spread over his chest, her eyes shut so that those ebony lashes fluttered against his cheek, her body close against his. So close that he thought he'd never be cold again.

"Tell me something," he murmured against her cheek.

She sighed. "Yes?"

"Do I really remember being in bed with a dog?"

Her chuckle vibrated through him like electricity. "We asked for volunteers."

Ian nodded. Kissed her again. "Next time I'll make provisions ahead of time."

She kissed him back. "Next time you won't have to."

Ian didn't exactly remember falling asleep after that. The last thing he remembered was Quinn's cheek against his chest, her hair tickling his neck. Her breathing soft and reassuring against him.

He awoke briefly sometime around dawn to find her back in her chair, curled up, her head resting against the back as if expecting to wake any second, as if she'd fought off sleep. He wanted to tell her to go to bed. He couldn't quite do it. It would have meant not being able to watch her, the morning sun warming her features and glistening in her hair. It would have meant he was alone again. It would have meant that he couldn't imagine any longer what it would be like to always wake up to her.

But Ian knew where that would lead him. One way or another, he was going to have to end up telling her the truth. And he knew well enough by now what it would mean.

He'd dealt with disappointment all his life; his family's disappointment in him, his in most of the rest of the world. He could certainly do it again. But somehow in the fresh light of morning, lying so close to a woman who could make him forget who he was and what he would become, he'd almost thought he could forget.

He could not. Fighting a new depression, he closed his eyes on her sleeping form and slipped back to sleep.

Seven

If anybody noticed that Quinn wasn't paying proper attention to her work, they weren't saying. No one had mentioned the fact that she wore the same outfit two days in a row, or that she'd not only missed one entire twenty-four-hour period while she'd battled the enigmatic Mr. Matthews into remission, but disappeared with amusing regularity to check in on him while he slept during the second twenty-four.

Even the colonel seemed hesitant to broach the subject. It seemed that once given the proper direction, she'd headed off on Mr. Matthews's care like an avenging angel. And the good colonel wasn't about to interfere with what he considered women's work.

Quinn didn't hear any of the speculation. She was too tired. She'd slept not at all the night before and spent a good deal of the ensuing day making sure that Ian would, in fact, wake up again. She wasn't used to malaria, after all. How did the colonel know for sure that Ian wouldn't develop those vicious convulsive chills as precipitously as he had before? How did he really know that Ian wouldn't spike another lethal fever, screaming out in pain and thrashing with an energy that was unnerving, only to lapse into a silence so profound that Quinn had to lay her hand on his chest to make sure he was breathing at all.

He didn't eat more than broth the entire day. When she checked in on him after ignoring her own dinner, she found him still asleep. Curled up, the sheet and blanket fallen to his waist, his hair tangled and tumbling into his eyes.

For the first time, he actually looked as if he were going to live. There was a little color in his cheeks, and he looked like someone who was resting rather than waiting for his place in line at the pearly gates.

Quinn was surprised that the realization would spark the sharp ache of tears. She didn't care enough for Ian to weep for him. How could she, if she still didn't know anything about him?

Not that she hadn't tried. While he'd slept she'd rummaged through every piece of clothing, every personal article in the room. She'd even checked his car. Everything supported his identity. Ian Matthews, home address sixteen Highgate Terrace, Kensington. Title, VP City Branch, Heritage House, Ltd. Tailors Anderson and Shepard on Saville Row, bank Barklay's, social friend, solicitor the Hon. Cecil Aubrey-White. Countries visited, France, the U.S. and Australia, three times. Passport picture atrocious. All quite normal.

Except that there were no military memories. No old school mementos. Nothing here about home and hearth. Except for one picture, taken in one of the ubiquitous gardens around the country, of a rather square, bluff-looking young man with his arm around a pretty smiling girl. Family? Friends? Impostors?

"Did you ever get to sleep?"

Quinn was startled from her reverie by the soft rasp of Ian's voice. She couldn't help but smile. "Playing possum, huh?"

"Doing a quick road test of the equipment before it's put into use. I will accept volunteers to help in a few...variations."

Quinn's grin was bright and irreverent. "Copenhagen is sleeping right outside the door. I'm sure he'd be happy to help."

Ian stretched carefully, grimaced, and resettled into much the same curled-up position. "Thank you, no. I find he's not quite my cup of tea."

"Well, thank God for small favors."

This was ridiculous. She wanted to giggle, to smile constantly the way her mother had once when her father had successfully awakened in intensive care after surgery. The relief that Ian was clear-eyed was actually palpable, like a sharp light in her chest where only a weight had resided.

She wanted to crawl back onto that soft, marshmallow bed with him. She wanted to touch his body and feel the health seep back in. She wanted to snuggle back into his embrace and listen to him hum "Greensleeves" to her the way he'd done deep in the night.

"Well," she offered with an assessing eye, "as Alistair might say, it doesn't quite look like you're going to succumb anymore. Are you getting hungry?"

His expression said it all. "Tomorrow, maybe. I find that interrogation is survived much better on an empty stomach."

She tilted her head at the lopsided smile that changed his features completely. "All right," she acknowledged, fighting to maintain her distance when all she wanted to do was sweep that hair out of his eyes and soothe the ache in his hip. "If that's the way you want it."

He seemed to consider it. "The way I want it," he finally decided, "is sitting up. But I rather think I'm not presentable."

Quinn had to laugh at that. She'd spent all of the previous day bathing him without benefit of "presentable," the only thing between them a washcloth and a little water. Suddenly he thought she needed protection from the facts of life.

Actually, Ian was lucky that Quinn had been too distracted by the numbers on that thermometer, the relentless thrashing and moaning that more than once had brought tears close enough to mingle with the cool water, to really worry about what she was doing. Or where. Or what that where looked like, because any other time she would have been breathing harder than Ian had been—and without benefit of protozoans in her blood.

What was even funnier was that sometime in the early hours when Quinn had been asleep, the colonel must have had the same thought as Ian, for he'd snuck in and remedied the situation by way of his own drawstring pajama bottoms, too wide and too short. Quinn motioned for Ian to take a look.

He lifted the sheet and grinned. "As efficient as ever, Miss Rutledge."

"Thank the colonel," she admonished. "He obviously thought I was in danger of swooning. Now then, do you want the chair, and I'll take the side of the bed?"

"I want a toothbrush," he said with some feeling. "There are some very vile beasties with felt feet residing on my tongue who need immediate eviction."

It took ten minutes longer than either of them expected, basically because Ian almost ended up on top of Quinn on the floor again. This time, though, Mary had nothing to do with it. His knees just kept buckling. He kept cursing, and Mary kept laughing. By the time Quinn had him settled back in the chair, he looked refreshed and she felt like a wrung-out rag.

The bed looked more appealing than even Ian, but Quinn held off. She had important business to attend to.

"All right," she said, trying her best to keep her eyes from wandering to Ian's still-bare chest. The dark golden hair there fanned into swirls and then trailed down to that tantalizing line that beckoned below the waistband of the pajamas. Quinn jerked her eyes northward and steeled herself. "What am I going to find when I call Lady Allison?"

Ian didn't seem in the least surprised. "That I'm just who I say I am. A middle-management type with a flair for tripping over romantic ruins on my regular hikes."

"Which just means that you have connections, because I don't believe you."

He nodded. "As well you might not. The only thing I know about renovation is that it costs buckets of money and that the parent company sees fit to charge exorbitant rates to its clients—guests—in order to seek recompense."

Quinn couldn't prevent a small grin and a shrug. "Actually, you probably have it down better than some of the people at corporate. Only they don't have a gun. At least not one that has fewer than two barrels."

"Don't you want the colonel in on this?"

"I'll let you know. You weren't in the Green Jackets, either, were you?"

He actually looked wistful, as if she'd tapped a special memory. "You guessed that, too?"

She shrugged. "Last I heard, they weren't into antiterrorist training. I don't even believe they have interrogation training. At least not the kind that leaves you blindfolded out in the middle of Wales for twelve hours to soften you up."

"You obviously have an opinion on the subject."

"Special Air Service?"

He nodded. "Bravo. The SAS isn't exactly a branch many Americans are familiar with."

"Still in it?"

His smile grew grim. "No," he admitted. "The hip was my ticket out."

"Brian was one of your team?"

He looked startled. "I'm going to have to be careful about whom I succumb to fevers around."

Quinn knew it wouldn't do to question him about that. She'd heard enough during those horrible dark hours. A friend killed. Slowly. Dreadfully. Ian impotent to stop it. There had been a rage in him Quinn didn't think was possible. A heart-rending anguish that made anything she'd ever faced child's play. She hurt all over again for him.

"So, who do you work for now?" she asked instead, and was pleased to see the flicker of relief in his eyes.

"London Police CID."

Quinn had rarely been dumbstruck. That did it. "Scotland yard? Good Lord, what for? Mary's been dead for over three hundred years. And as far as we know, nobody killed her— although there are certainly times it's a temptation to try."

Ian's smile was bright and rueful. Quinn was distracted by it.

"Actually I'm in more the preventative maintenance branch," he admitted. "I've been temporarily assigned to the Royalty Protection Department. Rather like the protection branch of your American Secret Service. We're assigned family members to watch."

Quinn made a point of looking around. "Not another prince looking for alternative life experience?" she demanded playfully. "Good heavens, can't that woman keep those kids under control?"

Ian had the good grace to smile. "Not here. Coming. I'm here to do a preliminary survey with which to plan protection."

"But I hadn't heard about this," she protested, automatically jumping up for her appointment book. Sitting back down just as quickly. "Good God, this is going to be the biggest thrill of Alistair's life!"

Ian leaned forward and took hold of her wrist. "Which is precisely why I've remained undercover, as it were. No one can know about this. No one. It's vital to security."

Quinn blinked, trying to understand. "But why not?"

"Because we're also having the delegations from Q'rat and Barouet here to discuss ending the hostilities between them."

Quinn couldn't decide quite what to say. "You're kidding," was all she could finally manage. Q'rat and Barouet had been fighting for years, small, oil-rich bedouin countries that could well squeeze off a good deal of the world's oil supply in their rush to choke each other out of Allah's favor.

There had been rumors in the news lately, word leaking of weary sheiks and frustrated kings. But just as many fanatics still held the line on either side, so that negotiations could easily prove to be precarious in the most physical sense.

"But I don't understand. What in God's name would the prince be doing at a meeting like that? He's not allowed to be anywhere near a real political situation."

Ian shrugged. "King Failel wouldn't agree to setting foot in a country that didn't have royalty." His sudden grin was irreverent. "I have the feeling he doesn't think anyone else would know how to pay him proper deference. Anyway, he has begged that someone from the royal family be there, at least to greet him. The various oil-dependent nations have added weight to the request. It seems that the king may very well have nuclear capability. They desperately need time to defuse a very hot situation."

"So the prince is going to be host for a group of Middle Easterners who each control some very testy terrorists, and they're all going to have a little chat at Hartley Hall."

Ian nodded. "That's about the size of it."

Quinn was on her feet before she knew it. "Are you crazy?"

"The security arrangements are quite thorough," he retorted with maddening ease as he leaned back in his chair.

Quinn decided she needed to pace. "Mary's waited three hundred years for an opportunity like this. The royal family right under her nose." Quinn stopped and leaned toward him, her message intent, her conviction rock solid. "How long do you think you're going to have your job when your boss falls bum-end down into another of her surprises—that *is* the one who's your charge, right?"

Ian nodded, clearly undisturbed. "Right."

She whirled around again. "And then, of course, there's the fact that in delicate negotiations, the last thing you need is somebody laughing out of turn. Especially when it's going to be difficult to convince the king that Mary's not laughing at him—because she probably will be!"

"I've relayed those very concerns to the head office. They're still convinced that Hartley Hall is the proper place to hold this meeting."

"Why?" Quinn demanded.

"Because of the fact that nobody would expect it here. The hall won't even be officially open when the delegates arrive. There's a lovely lawn out there to land helicopters on, enough isolation for anybody, masses of room for the various dignitaries to wander around and, as far as I can tell, fairly good defense against attack. And not everyone believes in ghosts."

"Attack?" she countered, coming to a dead stop in front of the chair. "My hall? Attacked?"

"Ah." He nodded. "Now we're at the meat of it. I imagine you're envisioning mortar rounds lobbed into the dining hall. Smoke grenades in the Gainsborough salon."

Quinn actually had to close her eyes. "Don't," she begged. "I can't stand it."

Ian took hold of her hand, now comforting her. "Quinn," he soothed. "We'd hardly allow something like this to be set up without making a thorough consideration of the ramifications."

Quinn still wanted no part of it. Opening one eye, she leveled a baleful glare Ian's way and was furious to see that he was smiling. "And just what do you plan to do about the ramification who throws books and drops trap doors?"

That actually had him thinking. "I'm still trying to work that out."

Quinn scowled. "And how long do we have to defuse all these little 'ramifications'?"

His smile was almost sheepish. "Two weeks."

She sucked air in like a vacuum. "There's only one person organized enough to make that possible."

"And I'm still not feeling up to snuff."

She didn't even grin at him. "And before we go talk to him, you might as well tell me—is the rest of your story true? Or do I need to know more?"

Ian's smile was easy and convincing. "What's the matter?" he asked. "Doesn't marriage to a vicar's son appeal to you?"

"Stop that," she snapped, yanking her hand away. "Are you telling the truth?"

"Yes. Everything I said, except for the job and the military career."

"Promise."

He held up his hand. He smiled. And he lied through his teeth. "On my word."

"Here?" the colonel echoed, slowly sitting down on the Adams chair as if his legs wouldn't hold him. "The prince is coming here?" His agitation was so great that his mustache took on a life of its own. Those great hoary eyebrows danced like caterpillars on a string.

"You don't suppose he'd be bringing . . . her, do you? It would do these old bones good to bow over that dainty little hand."

"No," Ian admitted, doing his best to keep a straight face. This was going to be worse than even Quinn had thought. "I'm afraid she couldn't make it. Besides, we wouldn't want to endanger any more of the family than necessary—although she offered, of course."

The colonel nodded, as if he were in her trust. "Of course. But the young man, he volunteered for this, didn't he? Just like him, of course. Has a backbone like his father, he has. Good military man."

Ian did his best not to sigh. He refused to look at Quinn, who was valiantly keeping a straight face. They'd waited until morning, when both Ian and Quinn had felt a bit more rested, to deal with the colonel. Now Ian wasn't sure they'd waited long enough.

Sometimes he forgot just what the old army was like. It had been why he'd forfeited a plumb commission in the Coldstream Guards to volunteer for the SAS, much to his family's eternal chagrin. Ian had been raised on queen and country, and gave proper respect to both. His military career had been preordained, just as it had been for the past twelve generations of second sons, give or take a rogue or two. But he'd stifled under the traditional system the colonel revered more than his own family. Ian had never been, would never be, a proper military man. Which was what had made him so perfect for the SAS.

But, of course, that was another time and place altogether. What he needed to do was get on with the job at hand. Lay out what he could for the colonel without giving away too much. Without offering him the information that would betray the rest of his own secret. The most damning secret.

"Right, then," the colonel suddenly boomed in his best parade-ground voice. "What is it needs to be done?"

"We need to find the rest of Mary's tricks, Sir Alistair," Quinn said.

The old man thought about it. He rubbed at his nose and then tugged at his mustache, as if the actions were part of the process for squeezing out thought. Quinn sat perfectly still beside Ian and waited, her face absolutely placid, her hands in the lap of her royal-blue jumpsuit.

Ian wanted to forget the old man. He wanted to turn to Quinn and talk about holidays or history or Kansas. He wanted to soak in the warmth in those life-giving brown eyes and wallow in the memory of waking up in the darkness with her dozing alongside him. Never leaving, patient, kind, her forehead pursed in anxiety and her hands as cool as spring air.

A stupid reason to fall in love. But still, he couldn't think of a better one. A brilliant creative mind linked to a compassionate soul. In his usual circles, something completely unheard of. He also couldn't say he minded the luminous, exotic looks.

Suddenly the colonel looked up. "Need a bit of fresh air, what? Join me?"

Both Ian and Quinn reacted with some bemusement. The colonel tilted his head toward the ceiling a few times, his eyes wide with meaning. Ian nodded with a wink. Good Lord, the old man didn't want the ghost to overhear him, and Ian was going right along with it. If his father saw this, he'd have him dispatched posthaste to the giggle farm.

"I'd like to see Blackie," Ian offered, getting gingerly to his feet. He still felt like left out pudding, a bit congealed and wobbly.

"Fine," the colonel agreed, snapping to his feet as if the prince had arrived early and throwing open the French windows. "Bloody-minded pig, that animal. How do you know him?"

Quinn surreptitiously slid her arm through Ian's as they followed Sir Alistair out into the sunshine. Ian smiled his gratitude. A perceptive, discreet woman. All this and heaven, too.

"Had the chance to ride him a few times," he allowed, folding his hand over Quinn's and proceeding as if they were taking a stroll through Hyde Park on a Sunday afternoon. Next he'd be buying her violets and arranging a carriage ride. He was hopeless. "The late viscount was rather generous with a rank amateur like myself."

"Dreadful shame, that," Alistair commiserated. "Fine young man, Giggleswick. Lived life to the fullest, though. It must have crushed the earl to lose him so young."

"He was the Earl of Malham's heir?" Quinn asked. "How did he die?"

"Bad judgment," Ian replied. "He went skiing with the wrong prince and ended up under a couple tons of snow."

Ian could tell that Quinn wasn't sure whether to grin or scowl at him. He didn't blame her. That was a common reaction. But then, the late viscount had earned every raised eyebrow; he'd been long on impulse and very short on personality or intelligence. Nigel the Twit, he'd been called.

"You were allowed to compete when you were in the Greens?" the old man asked.

Quinn was about to correct him, since they hadn't really got around to much more than Ian's present occupation, when Ian squeezed her hand. She looked up, confused, and Ian shook his head.

"Let's leave it go for a bit, shall we?" he asked. He knew she'd get the wrong impression, that she would connect his request with his previous one. That didn't really matter. Ian just knew that the minute the colonel began piecing together Ian's career, he'd remember much more than Ian wanted. He'd remember Ian's real name, and then the rest of Ian's story.

So when Quinn smiled and squeezed his hand in response, he felt like a bloody heel. He felt like the coward he was. But for just a little while longer, he wanted to think she could smile at him that way just because he was a civil-service worker with a limp.

"The regiment was very supportive," Ian lied baldly. "Especially when I was stationed close enough to make the meets. I'm afraid I enjoyed the sport much more than it enjoyed me."

He'd lived for it. Those few minutes, the dirt flying in his face, his shoulders screaming for rest, his nose full of mane, had been his freedom. He would never again experience the singular exultation of carrying Black Pagan over that last fence at Cheltenham, and on bright days like this, it ached in him.

Blackie saw them coming. Whinnying like a spoiled child left alone too long, he galloped straight for the fence. Ian ignored him. The colonel stood his ground just because Ian was. Quinn was looking at them both as if they'd lost their minds.

Blackie pulled up just short of disaster, kicking up dirt and arching his fine neck just far enough over the fence to take a swipe at the top of Ian's head. To Ian it felt like coming home.

"So, what do we do?" he asked the colonel.

Quinn was shaking her head now. "You must be in the right job," she marveled. "You have a complete disregard for personal safety."

Ian waved her off. "I knew just how far Blackie would come."

"I hope you have as much luck with Mary," the colonel huffed, pulling out a handkerchief to wipe a suspiciously pink visage.

"Because?" Quinn prompted, ever patient.

"Because," the old man echoed portentously as he stuffed the handkerchief back in his jacket pocket, "the only way we're going to find all those traps is to have Mary show them to us."

Ian knew he didn't want to ask the question. Even his job didn't require deliberate self-destruction. But that was just what he had the feeling he was walking into.

"And how do we do that?" he asked anyway.

The colonel looked back and forth between the two of them. "By making her very angry at us, of course."

Eight

———

"**I** don't think I like the sound of this," Quinn protested.

"Just what did you have in mind?" Ian asked, leaning once more against the rail. Neither Alistair nor Quinn followed suit, especially since Blackie was sidling back up to them.

Alistair stuffed his thumbs in his vest pockets and rolled a little on his heels. "Well, there are a score of things that will set the old girl off," he began. "Kipling and Cromwell, as we know. Elizabeth I, the Inquisition, Beethoven—"

"Beethoven?" Ian echoed.

Alistair harrumphed. "She prefers madrigals and baroque."

"Of course."

Alistair eyed Ian speculatively. "She doesn't seem overly fond of you."

"Then why is she trying to hook me up with him?" Quinn demanded.

Alistair's eyebrows danced again. "Blast if I know."

Ian seemed to be ignoring them both. "So we read Kipling out loud while playing Beethoven? Be rather like a bad school program."

"Oh, I don't think that would work," Quinn answered, since Alistair seemed suddenly too preoccupied by the proximity of Blackie's teeth to the top of Ian's head to do it. "She has to be really inspired to do something new. Like the time she sent the developer who wanted to turn the hall into a golf course through the library wall."

Blackie sidled a little closer, his mouth opening. Without even looking away from his conversation, Ian reached over his shoulder and batted the horse right on the nose. With a whinny, Blackie reared and turned away.

"I have it!" Alistair declared, hands together in jubilation.

Quinn almost flinched. He was sounding uncommonly jolly again.

"How do you think she'd react to being ignored?"

Quinn squinted at him. "I ignore her all the time."

"No, no. Her advice. The legendary matchmaking." Alistair was leaning forward now. Quinn suspected that had she been a man he would have been poking a finger in her chest. "I dare say that if you and Ian began to vilify each other in public, she'd be passionately insulted. Especially if Ian began arguing about the fact that no Irishwoman was going to run his life."

"Because she was an Irishwoman," Ian conceded.

"And she did run everybody's life," Quinn finished.

"Brilliant idea, old man," Ian agreed. "When do we start?"

Quinn took Ian's still-pale color and weary lines into consideration along with her own trepidation of Mary's formidable talents. "Are you sure we're up to this?"

Ian turned a dazzling smile on her. "Just think," he coaxed, "we can find out ahead of time just how to carry on a proper row."

"I already know, thanks."

"You can call me every name you've wanted to since I walked in the door."

She knew her neck was changing colors again. He saw it, too, because his gaze dipped to the base of her throat and then returned to hers, suddenly intimate and fond.

She did her best to make her smile wry. "Well, I have to admit that I'm coming up with some excellent ideas right now."

"Good show," Alistair approved, clapping Ian on the back with a bit too much enthusiasm. Ian almost landed on his face in the dirt.

Amusingly enough, it was Blackie who defended him. The big horse leaned way over the fence and butted the colonel squarely in the back. Alistair jumped as if he'd been shot. Far be it for Quinn to point out that a career cavalry man had no business being intimidated by a horse. She just dipped her head so Alistair didn't see the grin that wouldn't fade.

"Well, tell me this," she said instead, still watching the toe of her tennis shoe as she dug it into the hard-packed gravel. "Even if we find all Mary's hot spots before the conference, how do we make her behave during it?"

There was a certain amount of silent consultation about that, after which Alistair just shrugged. "Appeal to her sense of duty," he offered.

Quinn damn near laughed aloud. "Alistair, Mary never had a sense of duty. Except to the people who lived nearby."

"Appeal to that," Ian suggested. "Think of what would happen to the local populace if something untoward happened during the conference. They could actually be in physical danger if she does something that sets off one set of delegates."

"Then why have it here?" Quinn demanded yet again, hands on hips, eyes no longer down.

Ian's smile was at once knowing and apologetic. "The Earl of Malham offered the use of his latest Heritage House project, and his godchild accepted."

Quinn scowled. England, land of the Good Old Boy network. Well, it wasn't her problem, was it? She just had to make sure that the hall was at its most ready when the exalted guests began landing on the front park.

"Tell you what," she offered with all the good grace she could muster. "If we're not careful, Mary could set back renovations by months. Why don't we wait for act one until the workmen have gone?"

Alistair and Ian consulted again.

Ian nodded. "I would much rather not be dunked in an open bucket of Mostly Mauve, if it's all the same to you."

Alistair's laugh echoed out over the ocean, startling the birds. "Well done. We'll shut down operations at the close of the day."

"How about we give the workmen a day or two more?" Quinn asked. And Ian another forty-eight hours to recover, she thought. "The men were set to finish the plastering tomorrow, anyway."

Ian shook his head, unconcerned. "As long as the delegates can be assured of a warm meal and hot water, the wallpapering doesn't matter."

"Are you kidding?" she demanded. "Those men have at least three wives each, and every one of those women is going to have a comment about the furnishings."

Ian grinned. "No wives this trip. Just ferrets."

Both Quinn and Alistair stopped. "Just what?" Quinn asked.

Ian straightened away from the fence. "Ferrets. The king's pet...pets. He has four of them. Discovered them visiting Disneyworld, evidently, and can't be parted from them. Keeps the little beggars in gold cages and feeds them better than the royal corgis. He agreed to keep his wives at the Connaught for security's sake, but he goes nowhere without the ferrets."

Quinn just nodded, long since used to the vagaries of the wealthy. Jason's mother had bought a VCR for her poodle so the dear wouldn't miss Johnny Carson.

"Right, then," the colonel barked out, turning for the house. "Ready?"

"Sunday," Quinn insisted.

Both men stared over at her, and she realized that it would be anathema to the English military man to allow concession to overwhelming odds. Or the disabling effects of a very recent bout of malaria.

"Sunday," she repeated with just a bit more steel in her voice. "It's the day after tomorrow. Let me get the plaster in."

There was another brief conference between the two men accomplished entirely by eyebrow. One of these days, Quinn was going to have to learn how to do that.

Finally Ian turned back to her with a broad grin. "In that case," he announced, "I think I'd like to make the most of our last hours of compatibility." And before Quinn could say a word, he walked up and slid an arm through hers.

Quinn looked up at him, startled.

"Well," Alistair harrumphed without much enthusiasm. "I was wanting to go over security procedures and protocol with you..."

Ian's smile was brisk, efficient and phony. "Glad to. But later. Right now I'm in the mood for a walk on the beach."

It was Quinn's turn to object. "But Ian, I don't think—"

He silenced her with a smile. "Well, I do. Now, come on."

The steps down to the beach had been carved into the rock sometime in the eighteenth century. Quinn had had a handrail installed, so that the adventuresome would have an easier trek.

The sea was quiet today, swishing up on the beach like a hesitant breeze, the water a brilliant deep blue in the high sunlight. There were soft white clouds piled at the horizon, and a sudden stillness to the air the minute the cliff closed Quinn and Ian off from the rest of the world.

"You really shouldn't be hopping up and down steps yet," Quinn protested as they reached the sand.

Ian stopped a moment to take in the expanse of ocean before him, the corrugated coast of Cornwall marching away toward the horizon, the deepening beach in the isolated little cove and the boulders that hissed with receding water.

"I wasn't looking for exercise," he admitted, slipping out of his hacking jacket. "I was looking for privacy."

Quinn watched him spread the garment over the sand by his feet. Then he straightened and held out a hand. "Come sit," he offered.

For a moment Quinn hesitated. She felt so stiff and silly, like a young girl on her first date. A blind date at that. Ian wasn't the person she'd thought he was. He was a policeman. A very good impostor who had a history she wanted to know more about.

He also had a body she hadn't really minded cooling down. A body that under any other circumstances she would have been more than tempted to waste hours over. She caught herself wondering just what it would be like warming it back up again.

"Come on," he coaxed again, easing himself down onto the sand, his hand still up for her. "I promise not to bite."

Quinn grinned as she accepted his hand. "It's not you I'm worried about."

He was warm in contrast to the brisk air, his body hard and enticing beside hers. She drew her knees up and wrapped an arm around them, now even more uncomfortable. Excited, shy, anxious.

"A policeman, huh?" she said, wondering that her voice should sound quite so breathless. Amazed that she couldn't be a little more restrained. She was beset instead by the most giddy sense of headlong rush. A sled ride down an icy hill, a skimming trip on a sailboard, a free-fall for the few seconds before the parachute opened. Exhilaration, terror, anticipation.

Ian leaned back on one hand and bent his good leg up, his own attention on the empty ocean and the seabirds that dipped and wheeled above it. "Afraid so. Does that make a difference?"

Quinn thought about it. Her sudden grin betrayed her. "Yes, I'm afraid it does."

Ian looked at her, an odd darkness in his eyes. "Really? Why?"

Quinn chuckled. "A somewhat different kind of person than a middle-management executive," she allowed.

Ian conceded the point, still not quite smiling. "The money isn't nearly as good. The hours are worse."

"I imagine you travel a bit more."

"At least for now. That depends on whether or not I rejoin the regular force after my tour."

She looked over to see that he was far less offhand about this than she was, which set up a funny dance of excitement behind her ribs. They hadn't known each other that long. How could either of them be this serious?

But, she realized just as quickly, she was. Out of the blue, struck down by an inexplicable madness, torn right out of her well-planned, rigidly adhered-to career, her careful, controlled, single life. She was falling in love with a man she knew next to nothing about. And it was the most deliciously decadent insanity she'd ever experienced.

"What did you do before the Royalty Protection Department?" she asked.

He watched her, warily, she thought. "Murder investigations."

Her eyes widened. "Really. An ex-SAS . . . sergeant?"

"Captain."

She nodded. "Captain. I should have known. Now Chief Detective Inspector, or whatever, of Homicide and Royalty Protection Department of Scotland Yard. Impressive credentials."

Ian actually chuckled, his face relaxing just a millimeter. "Even second sons have to make something of themselves."

"Second sons of rural Sussex vicars."

"Um, yes."

She nodded again. "Does this mean the first son went into the family business?"

Ian's smile was once again private as he turned back out to the ocean. "Yes."

"Other family members?"

"One sister, married to a businessman. A few cousins and the like. You?"

"A sister and brother. They've never lived more than fifty miles from Ottumwa. Never wanted to. Six nieces and nephews between them."

"Do you see them often?"

She glanced at Ian, wondering how he would view her chronic wanderlust. "In between jobs. We're close, but we've never needed to be on each other's doorsteps."

He nodded, lifted a hand to tuck a strand of Quinn's hair behind her ear. "And you," he said, "have you ever thought about where you'd finally settle down?"

Quinn felt her answer catch in her chest, because the truth wasn't meant to be told quite so soon, that after all her years of traveling she had the sudden overwhelming urge to see what life would be like coming home night after night to open the same familiar door to the same well-loved face.

So instead, she looked down at her crossed legs, at the sensible tennis shoes she always wore while working on her houses. "How *does* one get a job protecting the odd prince and duke?" she asked, trailing her finger in the sand to make geometric patterns.

There was a moment of silence, the tug of the breeze her only answer, as if Ian were considering this change of tack.

"Rigorous selection processing," he finally answered. "Volunteering. And in some cases, a working knowledge of the family from hanging about with another second son during the Falklands."

"Ah," she acknowledged, still not looking up. "I imagine that helped the knack for fitting in."

"Fitting in?"

She looked up then, to see that he was still far too intent for comfort. He was going to get back to his question whether she liked it or not. All the same, his smile was disarming.

"I've been working for one of the most upper crust companies on the face of the earth," she countered, then paused to mimic Cecil Bagwhite's distinctive nasal tone with cruel precision. "There is the upper class, and the non-upper class. It would be unthinkable at Heritage House for one of our establishments to be mistaken for the latter."

Ian must have made Cecil's acquaintance after all, because the impersonation reduced him almost to tears. He ended up flat on his back.

"That could be deadly in the wrong hands."

Quinn's smile was smug. "Then I guess it's a good thing you don't work for Heritage House, after all."

"Yes," Ian agreed heartily, "isn't it?"

She thought of the last time she'd seen him on his back, asleep, vulnerable, as rumpled as a child. That sweet ache that had set up in her chest at the sight of him refused to recede.

"An old house," she finally acknowledged, her voice quiet.

Ian immediately looked over, the humor in his eyes gone, the ghostly gray suddenly piercing.

Quinn couldn't stop herself, even knowing that this was a watershed she was passing, even knowing that the intensity in Ian's eyes matched her own. "It doesn't have to be big," she said. "Just old. Well loved, with a lot of history imbedded in the walls and roof, so that if I close my eyes I can feel it shimmer around me. I can hear the laughter of generations of children, and maybe the Christmas carols they sang around the Yule log. I can smell the meat pies and lavender the lady used in her pomander. I can feel the continuity, the security, the timelessness of the place."

"Do you think you could share your house with a policeman who travels a bit?"

The sea shushed at her. The cormorants screamed and the sun dipped beneath a fast cloud. Quinn shivered, but it wasn't with the sudden chill of the wind. It was with the portent of permanence in Ian's eyes, the sudden seething heat that flooded that usually cool gray.

The air pulsed between them, turgid and sweet. Quinn couldn't seem to move, to breathe, to speak, to break the spell. Couldn't pull her gaze away from Ian's, because what they said in silence meant so much more than any words she could muster.

"Does the policeman already have any impediments I should know about?" she asked finally, her voice unforgiveably small with hunger. "Wife, children, gambling debts?"

She saw the smile and recognized his answering desire. His obvious conviction that should have terrified her. All it did was heighten the headlong rush, and the adrenaline in her bloodstream was like the fizz of champagne.

"No wife," he answered, and his voice was just as strained. Husky, deep. He reached out and took hold of her hand, pulling her down with him. "No children. No debts, except for the note on the Lotus and a bill from the bloodsuckers over at the hospital."

"Ex-anything?"

He shook his head. "You?"

She dipped her head a moment, her chest boiling with dread and exhilaration. She could feel the steady thrum of his heart through her fingertips. "Uh, yes. As a matter of fact, I do." Lifting her head, she tried to assess his reaction. "Does that make a difference?"

"I don't know," Ian retorted, his expression not much different, his hold still tight. Their faces were bare inches apart. "Does the gentleman resent new claims to your hand?"

Quinn's breath caught. "Are you?" she asked.

"What?"

"Claiming?"

He smiled, slow and warm and mysterious. "It is something to seriously consider, don't you think?"

She couldn't help it. She giggled. Raised a hand to her chest, as if that could contain the fierce exhilaration that made absolutely no sense. "I don't think after knowing each other less than a week, either of us has any right to use the word 'serious' about this at all."

Ian's eyes suddenly gleamed with the most unholy delight, and Quinn's exhilaration burst into joy. "So, in that case," he suggested, lifting a hand to wind it in her hair, "I shouldn't say that I seriously want to make love to you."

Quinn couldn't move. She couldn't seem to remember to breathe or blink or look away. Ian filled her entire comprehension, the sharp edge to his eyes, the taut ridge of his jaw, the way his fingers edged her closer to him. Her heart stumbled against his and her eyes grew unforgiveably wide.

"Probably not," she whispered, just before he brought her mouth down to his.

Soft. Fatally soft, as if those lips had been made just to protect her from hurt. Sweet. Unbearably sweet, addicting her from their first taste, until she couldn't seem to lift her head again, even if he wasn't holding her to him, which he was. Dangerous. Enough to make her forget the bright sunlight and the work that waited beyond that cliff and the future she'd mapped out so carefully.

"I shouldn't—" he continued, resetting them both until his other hand could test the pulse that throbbed at the edge of her throat "—tell you that you're seriously making me think of tossing those very practical work clothes of yours into the ocean and finding out what's beneath."

Quinn gasped as his fingers, callused and exquisitely gentle, slid along her collarbone to the hollow just above her breastbone. "No," she agreed, dipping back of her own accord for another taste of his mouth. "I imagine...you shouldn't."

It was silly. She knew the ocean was yards away, yet she could hear it inside, coursing through her, washing over her in waves of sensation, chills and fevers and glittering sparks like the sun when it struck fire off the crest of a wave. All from Ian's fingers. From his lips.

"And especially not," he continued, his lips testing the skin his fingers had first found, showering Quinn with new chills, "that I'm seriously thinking what fun we could have trying to have children."

Quinn's eyes were closed. She was arched against Ian like a cat against a soft quilt, kneading her fingers into him and stretching for his touch. Aching to feel that roughened fingertip against her nipple. Wallowing in the delicious intoxication of his hand in her hair.

"Children?" she gasped, writhing a little. Just to make him gasp, too, her one hand drifting much as his did. "Do you...want children?"

He smiled against her cheek, tickling her. She turned to his mouth and prevented an answer. Now completely drunk with the feel of him, with the heady exhilaration he was sparking in her. Mindless of consequence and responsibility and accountability.

He was a policeman, after all, not an executive. It was so much more enticing somehow. He had calluses he'd earned, and the rasp of them against her skin was decadent.

When he finally drew back from the kiss, he was almost as breathless as she. "Not . . . this very moment," he managed, smiling up into her eyes with enough suggestion to burn Quinn all the way to her toes. "Family wouldn't understand it just yet."

Quinn nodded, smiled with age-old promise. "All those vicars, I imagine."

Ian's chuckle vibrated through her.

"Good thing, though," she volunteered, anticipation finding its way into her voice as invitation. "Right now you wouldn't have any luck."

Quinn wanted to move again. She wanted to stop. She wanted Ian to find what was beneath the work clothes. Ian must have understood. Pulling her close, he rolled her onto her back, so that her head was nestled in the warm lining of his jacket and her legs stretched out on the cool sand.

She loved the weight of him on her, a solid, strong pressure that promised an intimacy she was sure she'd never get enough of.

"See?" she said with a slow smile. "I think you just like throwing yourself on the ground."

Ian trailed a finger down her cheek and along her jaw. "Especially if I can do it with you," he agreed.

His finger didn't stop at her jaw. It slid down her throat, past the hollow, down the breastbone to where her first button lay. Ian unbuttoned it. Slowly. Quinn didn't know whether to chuckle or groan.

"I find I've been wanting to do this since we met," he admitted, his eyes on his handiwork. The button undone, he bent to kiss the exposed skin.

Quinn made up her mind. She groaned. While he turned to the second button, she wound her own fingers in his hair. "I have to admit," she answered, her voice trailing as he succeeded with that button, too, "that I've had much the same thought. Especially when it was you, me . . . oh, and the washcloth."

He smiled again. This time his chin tickled her chest, and she squirmed beneath him.

"And to think I missed it," he mourned, and with one quick movement unsnapped her bra.

"Remind me later," she promised, quivering in anticipation of his touch, "to give you a demonstration."

Ian lifted his gaze to her, and it seared her. Quinn couldn't seem to get enough air when his eyes were on her. She couldn't seem to hold still. She couldn't think of the fact that it was broad daylight and the immutable truth was that she'd only known this man for less than a week. Those things suddenly didn't matter.

"You're beautiful," he breathed, his mouth quirked just a little, just enough to make his statement baldly honest.

Quinn had never been told that before. Not from a man who smiled as if surprised to hear himself say it. Not from a man who meant it as much as Ian did.

She couldn't answer, because the only words that came to mind were ones no man would want to hear yet. She couldn't tell him that she wanted to drown in his eyes and his touch for the rest of her life, that if he didn't keep his promise about making love to her she'd never forgive him—or herself.

"Do you hear bells?" he asked abruptly.

It took Quinn a second to answer. "I thought it was supposed to be fireworks and music," she offered weakly, hearing the ringing, too, and not wanting to answer. Not wanting to lose this precious hesitation in responsibility when all she had to think about was herself, when everything she'd never known she'd wanted seemed possible.

Ian managed a wry scowl, his hand still and his head lifted to catch the sound of the distant clang, clang, on the breeze.

"If I'm going to be transported enough to hear bells on the wind," he protested, "they are not going to sound like some ancient fire engine."

Quinn closed her eyes in defeat. The clanging went on, just as she knew it would.

"It's Alistair," she finally admitted, wishing with all her heart that one of them was the kind of person who could blithely ignore Alistair's discreet interruption. "There's an important phone call. That's how he calls me back when I wander off."

Ian lifted amused eyebrows at her. "You do this often?"

Quinn managed a scowl, still only inches away, yet suddenly farther, suddenly chilly with the dislocation of interruption. "Whenever I can coax a policeman onto the beach," she retorted dryly. "I'm especially fond of it after having nursed him through a bout of malaria."

Ian's smile was devastating as he bent down for a final heartfelt kiss that curled Quinn's toes in her tennies. "A health regimen I highly recommend," he agreed. "I'd be more than happy to give it another go later."

"Where?" she demanded. "The house is out. We'd be spoiling that Academy Award level performance Alistair expects from us."

Ian took a second to look around. "Here?"

"Tide's coming in."

"Well, surely there's a folly or two in the woods." He lifted a hand to brush back her hair, his fingers lingering long after they needed to. Quinn couldn't take her gaze from his, steeping herself in that soft wry gray of his eyes, fascinated by the tiny shafts of blue that flared out from the pupils, thinking of those sable lashes against her cheeks.

"If there isn't," she promised, "we'll provide one."

This time he lingered over his kiss, and Quinn closed her eyes to savor the taste of him, the smell of him, the hard, rough feel of him against her skin. And realized that the bells she heard weren't anything like an old fire engine. They were more like wind chimes, sweet and melodic and enticing. Warning bells that she no longer paid any attention to.

But the other bell was still ringing, more insistently than ever. There finally wasn't anything they could do but answer it or face the prospect of Alistair's sending one of the workmen after them.

Ian demanded the pleasure of redoing what he'd undone and almost undid all of Quinn's hard-gained composure along with it. He picked up his jacket and brushed it off before slipping back into it, and then they walked hand in hand back up the steps to the house.

Alistair met them with red face and in high dudgeon.

"It's your office, man," he accused the minute he set eyes on them. "They said to get you immediately. Another threat has been received."

Quinn turned on Ian. "Another?"

But he had already let go of her hand and was heading into the house.

Nine

———

"Release *what* prisoners?"

Ian settled into the green-and-white-striped Chippendale chair and did his best to catch his breath and attention. He'd left Quinn outside the study with Alistair, knowing that he couldn't be distracted from this phone call.

"That's just the problem, old son," his caller objected in a frustrated drawl. "They weren't obliging enough to identify them. Just said, release the prisoners or suffer the consequences."

Rubbing at the bridge of his nose, Ian leaned his elbows on the secretary and stared blindly out the front drive where a twin line of oaks that predated the present royal family name marched along, tall, sturdy sentinals against a wind that had warped them all the same way. "Mailed from London."

"Just like the others. Plain bond paper, standard business envelope, letters cut from one of the glossy magazines."

"And you think it's legitimate."

"Afraid so."

If he thought it was legitimate, Ian had to listen. He was no longer dealing with dear Leila, who spent the majority of her time protecting her own position. Sir Basil Farquhar was the best, in the course of his career trained in everything from antiterrorist tactics to cryptography. Holder of the Victoria Cross, he'd been personally responsible for pulling more than one member of the royal family out of the line of potential fire.

And his opinion was that the conference set for Hartley Hall in less than two weeks was a powder keg. Well, Ian had dealt with powder kegs before. The secret was to make sure there was no detonator available.

"I hear you had a spot of trouble with the old ailment. I thought the medicos had given you a clean slate."

Ian sighed. "Boring," he admitted, his attention split between the unsigned note promising catastrophe and the memory of Quinn bent over him, murmuring, her hand cool against his forehead. He actually shook his head to drag his attention back to the matter at hand. And that had never happened to him before. "The plans will be to you by tomorrow. We're still trying to work out a few of the kinks."

"The, uh, colonel told me." The well-bred voice paused with some amusement, the typical upper-class prejudice against the unusual. "A ghost?"

Ian could do no more than concur. "A ghost." And a renovator. A slim, bright, obsessed keeper of other people's history who kept creeping back into Ian's thoughts and destroying his concentration. Who made promises with just her eyes Ian had never before wanted to have made. Who had fatal sensitivity and the most sensual mouth Ian had ever kissed.

The ghost, in the end, would be the easy part.

Ian rubbed harder at his nose. "Read me the note he received one more time."

"'Your Royal Highness. We know they are coming. You have compassion. Help us free the helpless prisoners, or the meeting will suffer the consequences.'"

Ian grunted. "Polite for terrorists."

"Quite."

"Must have mutilated quite a few mags for all that." If nothing else, he'd make sure Quinn was gone before the conference.

"Not very helpful, though. Both sides have camps full of prisoners."

Ian agreed. "Both sides have been cited for civil-rights violations. Well, it sounds as if you're just going to have to wait for another message to better pin it down."

"And you're going to have to exorcise a ghost." The voice was now vastly amused. Ian couldn't say he blamed him. "Spoke to Lady Allison the other day, by the way. She said to make sure you leave her renovations expert intact, or words to that effect."

Ian must not have answered quickly enough. Something like a chuckle came over the line.

"Does she know who you are and all that?"

"No. She just thinks I'm an enterprising copper who did his stint with the SAS and came out of the Falklands with a limp."

"But you—"

"I think I'd rather leave it the way it is, if you don't mind, old man," Ian suggested. "It's all so much less complicated this way."

Sir Basil's answer was another severely delighted chuckle and the driest of concessions. "Of course, my lord."

Ian winced and hoped nobody was listening on the line.

Quinn never knew she could enjoy a good fight so much. She'd been raised in a well-behaved household where arguments were carried out pianissimo and disagreements brushed carefully under the rug until doors were closed. Somewhere in her insecure years, she'd forfeited the urge to challenge, always vaguely plagued by the feeling that if she was too much of a nuisance her parents would simply send her back and ask for a refund.

It hadn't been until she'd found her passion in renovation that she'd actually had the courage to stand up for her beliefs. And that, of course, had been done carefully. Civilly. She'd never known the pleasure of pulling out all the stops and being a raging bitch.

She was finding out that it was great fun.

"You listen to me, you pompous, middle-class pretender to a prig," she howled at Ian from the other end of the hallway with the result that it echoed with great effect. "You can take your manners and shove them where the sun don't shine!"

"How dare you!" Ian snapped back, stomping her way, his mannerisms exaggerated enough to make Quinn want to giggle. "Do you know what I can do to your career?"

Quinn laughed. "Don't overestimate yourself, Chauncey. Just because *you* think you're wonderful doesn't mean that anybody else does!"

Toe to toe, they glared at each other, long past the initial fuel that had set off the second or third round of arguments. This one, if Quinn remembered correctly, had something to do with Quinn's deplorable lack of concern about proper social form.

Ian straightened to his full height, and Quinn saw something new in his posture, something reminiscent of Alistair in full battle cry, that old regimental pose, eyes peering down at her from along his nose, chin tucked in, back so straight it almost bowed out the other way. She could almost imagine his heels clicking.

"No wonder you're to that benighted Irishwoman's taste," he hissed.

Quinn lifted her head to match him stare for stare. "The question is," she retorted, "why in God's name, you are."

Silence, ringing through the house, punctuated by the resonant ticking of the clock far down the hall.

"Are you going to show me the cellars?" he grated.

She never relaxed. "As quickly as possible."

It would be, they'd decided, in the original area of the house that they would find the last of the traps. They'd already managed to incur enough wrath the day before to discover that the banister to the great stairs, which Quinn had thought eminently safe, since they'd completely removed it to refinish the wood, had a tendency to sink suddenly if leaned on the wrong way. Ian had caught himself just shy of tumbling arse over end.

Today they were going to inspect the area where the surveillance equipment would be situated in the wine cellar and the Dungeon Snug, as the brochures would call the little bar set back into the arching stone that supported the house.

The steps down to the cellar were stone, worn into concave smoothness from centuries of passing feet. As everywhere else, electricity ruled the day, but the shadows had been ingeniously maintained to provide atmosphere.

Halfway down, Quinn automatically ducked. "Watch out for the—"

She was too late. She heard the dull crack and turned to see Ian down on his backside rubbing his forehead.

"—overhang," she finished with a rueful smile. "It was one of Mary's favorites."

The overhang was six inches lower than the surrounding roof, sure to catch the unwary and provide pratfalls, not to mention protect Mary's valuables collected in the recesses of the farthest room from impetuous invaders.

"You did that on purpose," Ian snarled, although the telltale sparkle never left his eyes.

Quinn's smile was now bright and unapologetic. "Whatever you think," she agreed and turned away.

Even more than fun, the fights were exciting. Stimulating. There had been a couple of times when they'd been face-to-face that she'd been sure Ian was going to just pick her up off the ground and haul her up to one of the bedrooms. There had been a couple of times when she'd been desperate for him to. He wasn't at all hard on the eyes when he was in a temper.

The air had sparked between them, hot and close and sizzling, the tension something completely different than anger, and it had been all Quinn could do to keep up the masquerade.

"This is the Dungeon Snug," she announced, flipping on another set of lights. "The perfect place for that late-night get-together."

The corner was indeed snug, tucked away beneath one of the arch supports, with an old leather-and-mahogany bar and several small tables and leather chairs scattered over the stone floor. Medieval weaponry and implements of torture hung from the walls, and behind the bar, hanging glasses would gleam from the lights.

Ian snorted. "I thought they said you had taste."

Quinn spun on her heel, the slur inciting instinctive reaction. "You suddenly seem to find fault with everything I've done."

"Not suddenly," he answered. "It's just that I'm growing very weary of your all-knowing attitude. You Yanks do have the idea that you're the arbiters of taste and history, now, don't you?"

"Far be it for me to blow a fresh breeze into a society so stuffy it hasn't introduced a new dish into its cuisine in two hundred years. You're right, though. Who'd think to decorate a dungeon bar with maces? I should have been bold and gone with French Provincial."

Ian did one of those tip-to-toe assessments that would have frozen the unwary on the spot. Quinn never took her hands from her hips.

"Well, there's one good thing," he drawled in the most offensive manner possible. "You won't be able to ruin Kinsale if they give it to you. The Irish have just about as much taste as the Americans."

That should do it. Quinn almost ducked right on the spot. She could hear the sound of wind, a moaning that seemed to swell from the stone itself. Mary working up a good frenzy.

"I wouldn't say much more about the Irish in Mary's house," she warned, half-serious.

Ian's supercilious attitude never changed. He looked way down his nose at her again. "Don't be absurd," he snapped, walking toward the wine cellar. "The Irish haven't won a fight against an Englishman in over three hundred years."

Opening the door, he flipped the light switch. And promptly disappeared.

It took Quinn a moment to realize it.

"Ian!" she yelled, running after him.

The wine cellar was half-stocked, the bottles snug in their tiers beneath the glare of fluorescent lighting. The floor was solid, the walls unmarked and the ceiling arching perfectly above Quinn's head. The room was empty.

"Ian!" she yelled again, suddenly really frightened.

"In here," she heard faintly, and it seemed to be coming from the rack of wine to her left.

"Where?" she demanded, running a frustrated hand over the wooden framing.

"Inside."

She felt as if she'd reached the rabbit hole just behind Alice. There was nothing to see that might point to Ian's location, yet she could hear him, his voice echoing distantly in the stone.

And then, of course, there was the laughter. Full-throated and delighted, bouncing off the stones like live ammunition. Quinn kept running her hands along the old wood, searching for purchase, wondering how the workmen had restored the racks without discovering Mary's trick.

Quinn earned nothing more than a splinter in her palm for her efforts. "I should just leave you in there," she snapped, sucking on the splinter before she yanked it out. "It'd serve you right."

"I say," Alistair said on a huffing run behind her. "Spot of trouble, what?"

Quinn turned to find him preceded by Copenhagen. Their defense mechanism, kind of like the flag of truce used to get the injured off the field of battle. The Great Dane trotted right up to the far-left rack of wine and began pawing at it. It was Mary who howled.

"There's a good chap," Alistair praised the dog and bent to help. Something they did worked, because suddenly the shelving sprang forward and pushed Ian out like a jack-in-the-box.

"She was waiting for me," he objected, dusting off his once-spotless gray flannel. "The shelves were already open. They slammed me inside the minute I walked in the door."

There was enough room in there for one adult or two small children, Quinn figured, a hidey-hole with a view through the wine. Perfect haven or jail.

"Are you all right?" Quinn couldn't help asking.

For a split second Ian's response was an honest one. His eyes warmed and his hands came up. The warning in Alistair's eyes must have been enough, because with his hands still out, he froze, his posture straightening again, his eyebrows lifting.

"No thanks to your benefactor," he answered, looking vaguely upward to the laughter that echoed more distantly, as if Mary had lost interest now that Ian had been freed.

"She shouldn't have to listen to you making fun of her in her own house."

He kept dusting off his clothing as he limped toward the stairs. "Silly nit. To think people take her advice."

"Does that mean," Quinn asked, following in his wake, "that I won't be expecting a proposal from you?"

He didn't turn around, but Quinn could read his expression from just the way he carried his shoulders. It almost made her smile.

"I do not take marital advice from ghosts," he answered stiffly, his shoulder tight against the laughter he was fighting. "Especially itinerant Irish ones."

There was only one thing Quinn could say to that. She fought a grin and said it. "Good." And kept her eyes open for the next trap.

* * *

Ian felt vaguely silly waiting until he was in the village just to make a phone call. No matter what proof he'd been subjected to in the previous few days, he still balked at the idea of worrying about a ghost overhearing his conversations.

But there it was. He was doing it, sliding into a phone kiosk at the top of the High Street with a full view of Gwynnup Green laid out before him, the tangle of white and red houses, the serpentine streets, the tumble of flower boxes, the sharp green of the rounded meadows and there, caught between the two arms of the headland, the silver glint of the sea. A place where he'd been seen as no more than a businessman, where nothing had been expected of him simply because of his name, no distance maintained, no favors fawned for. The Green would always stay a special place to him for that, even if it hadn't given him Quinn, as well.

"Ian, dear, you're not making any sense."

Smiling with huge satisfaction, Ian turned back to his conversation. "I said, Mama," he repeated briskly, "that you can call off the next round of prospective brides. I've found her."

"You've found whom, dear? You've only left here last week. And you're in Cornwall, for heaven's sake."

"Yes, I am," he agreed heartily. "Beyond reach of every Gwendolyn and Caroline in the kingdom."

"Ian, I won't have it. You've been perfectly beastly about Gwendolyn. She was your brother's fiancée, after all."

"And he was welcome to her," Ian retorted. "But I think I'd like someone a bit more interesting."

There was a pause, during which Ian could hear the dogs fighting in the background. He was lucky he'd caught her in. Tuesday was the Quorn. She should have been out chasing small furry animals over impossible hedges on a horse that cost more than most fisherman here pulled in in a year.

"It *is* someone we know, of course," she finally said, her voice showing the first signs of concern.

"Not at all," he answered. "I've just met her."

"Oh, Ian," she protested. "That simply won't do. You're just not *anyone*, you know. Consider the repercussions."

He was thinking instead of the fun they'd had fighting, the exhilaration of seeing Quinn sparkling and sharp, her eyes saying one thing and her waspish tongue another. He was thinking of how very badly he wanted to keep his promise about making love to her.

He'd been thinking of that every minute of the past two nights, alone in that huge soft bed with nothing to keep him company but the relentless ticking of the clock downstairs, the sheets hot and crumpled, his body literally aching with unexpected need.

He was thinking of how long he'd spent evading his mother's persistent efforts at matchmaking only to fall like a callow schoolboy the minute he wasn't paying attention. And to the absolutely wrong person, as his mother was telling him. And he was thinking of how that delighted him all the more.

"She's American," he said instead, still smiling, still enjoying the view. "From Iowa. About twenty-six, tall, with dark hair and eyes, and several very impressive degrees."

"Her family..."

"She's not sure," he said. "She's adopted."

There was a slightly strangled sound from the other end of the line, then another pause. "Don't be absurd," she finally managed. "Of course, you may see her. Bring her round if you'd like, for a weekend. But, I simply don't think she'd... well, *do,* dear. Not for a wife."

"She'll have to," he assured her. "I'm asking her to marry me this week."

"Ian! Control yourself. I've already told you that Gwendolyn is a perfectly charming girl who would suit you quite well."

"For the final time," he said, thinking of mousy brown hair, dim intelligence and an ear-shattering giggle, "no."

He shouldn't enjoy this so much. He was devastating his mother, he knew. She'd be up in bed with a sick headache for a fortnight. If there was one thing she truly believed in, it was place. And it was not Ian's place to marry some adopted stranger from the wilds of middle America.

"This is madness," his mother protested.

"Yes," Ian agreed, "isn't it?"

"She'd only marry you for who you are."

"Not at all," he said, and this was the reason he knew he had to marry Quinn before she got away from him. "She'd marry me without having a clue as to who I am."

* * *

He had things to do when he returned to the hall. Official calls to make, reports to finish up, layouts to consider. It would be his job to suggest allocation of bedrooms, boardrooms, ancillary support areas and the like. Instead, he went in search of Quinn.

"Are you sure you should be up there?"

The question came out with much too much sincere concern, he thought distractedly, looking up at a most beguiling vision of corduroy-snug backside and long legs.

Quinn was perched at the very top of the rolling ladder that serviced the library that Mary had installed before libraries were fashionable. At the sound of Ian's voice below her, she turned with a quick smile.

"Hardly hazardous for a person who's been known to crawl around open battlements in a gale," she answered, sliding a book from the stack she carried under her arm onto the top shelf. It seemed precarious work to Ian, but she didn't seem in the least disconcerted.

"What goes on the top?" he asked, head still back, hands comfortably shoved in pockets, much too content with the view to move.

"Greek history," she allowed. "We figured nobody's going to be really interested enough to read it."

"Actually," he argued dryly, "educated sorts inhale the stuff."

She turned, her eyes sparkling. "You know from personal experience, I presume."

"Naturally. I absolutely quiver with anticipation at the thought of reliving every thrust and parry of the Peloponnesian Wars."

With deliberate ease, Quinn turned back to the shelving. "You would."

"And what do *you* find edifying?" he challenged.

She turned again, another book poised just above his head, her smile sharp with answering challenge. "The American Revolution," she said. "We won that one, you know."

"A popular misconception," he retorted. "We simply decided that we didn't wish to be saddled with a useless huge chunk of forest and tobacco."

"You undoubtedly had an ancestor in that one, too, huh?"

He couldn't help grinning. "A vicar or two, I suppose."

This wasn't the fight they were supposed to be having, he knew. They were supposed to be shrilling at each other, as they had been. Ian didn't particularly care. He wanted to continue this way, as quick and clean as a fencing lesson, as exhilarating as a close dance.

"Come down here," he said suddenly, surprisingly serious, his voice sharpened with the persistent memory of having Quinn's soft skin beneath his hands out in the sand. He most definitely wanted it in his hands again.

She turned wry eyes on him from fifteen feet up, shadowed by the soft lighting, laughing, and Ian fought his hunger like a starving man alone in the wilderness.

"Why?" she demanded, her voice saying one thing, her dark eyes another, filled with shared memory, shared desire.

"Because I find it boringly inconvenient to try to kiss a woman fifteen feet above my head. That's why."

She laughed, the bright bubble of sound cascading through the wood-and-leather room. "And I'm supposed to just fall at your feet at such an elegant request."

"Yes," he answered. "You bloody well are."

He hadn't meant it. Not literally. Evidently Mary took him at his word.

Ian's first hint that something was very wrong was the sudden shift in Quinn's expression, from smug to alarmed. She let out an odd little yelp and dropped the books she'd been clutching.

"Hey!" Ian ducked just in time to miss the heavy missiles as they clattered around him. He looked back up to see what Quinn must have felt. The entire section of shelving was pulling away from the wall. If Ian stood where he was, he'd be crushed beneath the weight of the wood, not to mention the ton or so of books that were already beginning to slide his way.

"Jump!" he yelled, backing up over the Oriental carpet.

Quinn hung on to that ladder like a climber clinging to the side of a mountain as the shelving tilted even farther, creaking and groaning all the while. Books began to thud to the floor, and Ian reached his hands up, still far short of her.

"Jump, damn it!" he yelled. "I'll catch you."

"You'll kill yourself!" she yelled back.

"Do it!"

She did. Twisting around on the dropping ladder, she pushed off with her feet and reached her arms out to Ian. She was light; Ian already knew that, but not light enough. Both of them went crashing to the floor just shy of one of the chair groupings. Ian cursed soundly with the sharp protest from his hip and Quinn echoed him, rubbing an elbow that had made contact with the floor.

Ian barely took the time to land before rolling them both farther out of the way before the shelves toppled on them. Books were still sliding and thudding onto the parquet flooring. The shelves were still screeching. Just as Ian and Quinn cleared the disaster area, the shelves stopped tilting.

"Bloody hell," Ian breathed, an eye to them as he wrapped protective arms around Quinn. He'd ended up on top in an effort to protect her from the worst. It looked, however, as if the worst would be suffered by his ego. The shelves, hinged halfway up, were held at an angle by another ancient hinged arm that had been tucked within the unit.

Mary's sudden laughter was hearty and much too self-satisfied.

"How did I miss that?" Quinn wondered from beneath Ian.

He turned to find her attention back on the shelving. "What was the trigger?"

"It started to come loose when I put up that last book. There must be some kind of catch up there." She turned those great soft brown eyes back to him, her forehead pursed with concern. "Are you all right?"

Ian remembered what he'd been thinking just before she'd so precipitously joined him on the floor, and he smiled. "Couldn't be better."

She was trapped there beneath him, her body soft and welcoming, her smile provocative, her eyes as hungry as his. Ian felt her heart skid and falter beneath him, heard the sharp surprise of her breathing. He slid his arms along her sides, holding her tight, capturing her for himself. The hunger in him hardened, and he knew she felt it. Her lips opened in response, in invitation. She ran her tongue over her lower lip, and Ian couldn't pull his gaze away from it.

"You're asking for trouble," he warned, his own breathing shallow, his own heart beginning to thud.

When she did no more than smile, he caught her head between his hands and sated his hands with her hair. She tilted her face up to him, and he kissed her.

Soft, he thought. Sweet, oh, so sweet. She was intoxicating, like a rich old brandy, heady to the senses even before tasted. And now, sipping at her, he reeled with the subtle flavor of her. The exhilarating warmth, a life to inhale, ingest, dipping his face to it, his lips, his tongue to roll it about and praise it. He stroked her skin with roughened fingers that sank into its velvet texture. He wove his fingers into her hair and thought of silk, dark, sleek silk that had been created to be touched. To be swept across the skin with a whisper as tempting as a promise.

He heard her whimper of pleasure as she brought her own hands up for purchase, and thought of music. Seductive, sensuous music to taunt a man's dreams and mesmerize him upon waking.

He wrapped himself in her and forgot the rest of the world.

It didn't forget him.

He didn't hear the padding of footsteps. He didn't even pay attention to the low keen of recognition. On the other hand, he could hardly ignore the very wet nose that nudged him in the ear.

"What the . . . ?"

Ian started. Beneath him, Quinn offered a heartfelt oath.

"Get out of here," Ian grated, pushing at the offender.

"He obviously thought that it was the Cromwell again," Quinn defended the dog, her body beginning to tremble with laughter. Reaching up beyond Ian she scratched at the dog's ears and was rewarded with a low moaning growl and Copenhagen's prompt company on the floor.

"This isn't what I had in mind," Ian snarled, when the dog inserted his snout right atop Quinn's chest. Ian didn't want to be a boor and say it should have been *his* snout there.

Quinn laughed again, the breathless sound driving Ian even closer to the brink of control. "I imagine the colonel will be in here next. We should probably . . . um, get up."

Ian struggled to control himself. "Is the tide in?" he demanded.

She met his gaze with one of challenge, bright, seething. "Yes," she said on a whisper.

The dog didn't move. Ian didn't move. Quinn didn't move.

"What about that folly?" she asked.

Ian thought about his assignment. He thought of the repercussions of what he was about to do, both to himself, his family and his country. And then he pulled himself up off the floor.

"Come on," he commanded, and pulled Quinn up after him.

Copenhagen sprang to his feet, but Ian turned on the dog with murder in his eyes, if not his heart. "And you'll bloody well stay here," he snapped.

Copenhagen sank right back down on the carpet.

Quinn laughed and followed, her hand firmly in Ian's.

Alistair met them in the hallway. "I heard a dreadful racket . . ."

Ian didn't even bother to stop on the way past.

"See to the library," Quinn told the old man, still laughing.

"I say," he protested, turning after them. "I don't think this is quite what we had in mind."

"Alistair," Quinn commanded without turning back. "See to the library."

"Oh." The old man seemed completely nonplussed. "Quite."

Ian didn't care. For once in his life, he was going to do something that was for nobody's benefit but his. He was going to take Quinn upstairs and make love to her until one or both of them collapsed from exhaustion. And then, when they woke up, he'd start again.

Ten

Quinn knew better. She'd always known better. A practical child, a practical woman given to only one flight of fancy, and that quickly enough remedied when she'd realized she had married the wrong man for the wrong reasons.

She was not the kind of person to be dragged up to a bedroom. She didn't allow men to slam doors shut behind her without even giving her the choice to say no, thank you. She didn't get so weak at the knees with just a kiss and a set of seething gray eyes that she would risk everything just to fold herself back in his arms.

Which was why she was so amazed, because that was just what she was doing. She wanted Ian even more than he wanted her. She wanted to sink into his embrace, to spark fire with her fingers and provoke him to madness. She wanted to see Ian Matthews lose control, and she wanted to be the reason.

"I'm not sure this is the place you want to be," she demurred, however, when he opened the door to her bedroom.

He barely took the time to take in the early Victorian furniture, the chintz curtains and spread, the cabbage-rose wallpaper. "Why?" he demanded. "What's wrong with it?"

She actually giggled. "It's Mary's bedroom."

It took a moment for that to sink in. Quinn had never been uncomfortable sleeping here where Mary's presence was the strongest. But making love here might be pushing things a little. She was plagued by the feeling that someone was looking over her shoulder.

"You lied to me before," Ian accused with a grin.

"You bet."

Neither asked what had changed since that night at the pub. Both of them knew. Without another word, Ian took her once again by the hand and led her across the hall. To his room. Where she had nursed him, where she'd sat by him and bathed him and held him while he'd shouted and fought and wept. Where she'd begun to fall in love with him.

Quinn turned to him the minute the door was closed. Ian wasn't smiling now. His jaw was as taut as wire, his eyes dark. The intensity of his passion shimmered from him. It almost frightened her. She'd never seen him quite like this before, this close to losing control.

What she wanted. What she needed. What she wasn't sure she could handle.

It didn't matter. She met him there, at the foot of his bed, her hands cold with nervousness, her chest on fire with anticipation, her belly taut with hunger. She turned to him and smiled, and hoped that he could see how very much she wanted this.

"Are you sure?" he asked, his voice suddenly raw with waiting.

She didn't answer. Instead she took her hand from his and began to deliberately unbutton her blouse. She never dropped her gaze, never faltered before the yearning in his eyes.

"No," he whispered, stepping closer, pulling her hands away, lifting them both and kissing her palms. "Let me."

Quinn raised her hands to cradle his face, that face she had stroked and rinsed and memorized during the small hours of the night, and she looked hard into those hypnotic gray eyes.

"Are *you* sure?" she asked, and held her breath for his answer.

For a long agonizing moment, he only stared at her. Stood stock-still as if he couldn't quite form the words. Quinn waited, held on, the stubble of his new beard tickling her fingertips, the rise and fall of his chest felt as intimately as her own.

"Do you know what you're doing to me?" he rasped finally, pulling her into his arms. "I can't sleep and I can't think and I can't seem to get cold-enough showers."

Quinn let go of him and wrapped her arms around his neck. Her face pressed against his chest where she could hear the strong cadence of his heart, where she could absorb his strength. He bent his head over hers, wrapped his arms tighter, folded her so close she could hardly breathe.

"I want you," he whispered. "I'm falling in love with you, and there doesn't seem to be a damn thing I can do about it."

Quinn squeezed her eyes against the sudden tears his words incited. "I apologize for all the bother," she allowed, just as breathless, just as tormented. "But you're just as much at fault as I am. I haven't had any sleep since you hobbled up the front steps."

"In that case," he answered, lifting his head to look back down at her again. "Let's do something about it."

Quinn smiled for him, and the tears filled her eyes, anyway. "Oh, let's," she sighed, and sighed again when he bent back down to kiss her.

She loved the taste of him, dark, musky flavors of coffee and ale and brandy. She loved the feel of him, the satin torture of his lips, the rasp of his tongue, the sleek ivory of his teeth. She lifted onto her toes to fit better against him and let him ease her lips open, let him explore her back with his hands, let him pull her so close against him that she could feel the heat of his skin through his crisp cotton shirt.

He let go of her just enough to slide his fingers along the collar of her blouse. "You always...wear silk to shelve books?" he demanded without lifting his mouth from hers, his fingers reaching her buttons.

Quinn smiled, tremulous and shy, her own hands exploring beneath the cover of his tweed jacket, her skin skittering with the brush of his approach. The delicious rasp of coarse fingers against silk. She hadn't worn the blouse on purpose; she just liked silk. But suddenly Quinn couldn't ever imagine having Ian unbutton anything but silk against her skin. The sensations were too intoxicating, the whisper of silk in his hands maddening.

The buttons fell open, one by one. Her blouse gaped, exposing cream lace and the swell of her breasts. The air chilled her. His touch burned her. Quinn couldn't move, couldn't stay still against him, so anxious to have him find his way back to her, so hungry for those callused hands to seek out the slick heat that anticipated him.

She lifted her own hands, her fingers fumbling in her haste, to see what lay beyond that cotton and tweed. And as she sought, as she uncovered those taut, sleek muscles and the curl of golden hair she'd tried so hard to ignore when she'd had a washcloth in her hands, she gave her mouth to him, offered herself to be pillaged and plundered, gave up little moans of pleasure to mingle with his, tasting, sipping, teasing, teeth and tongue testing the soft swell of a lip, lips rasping across the delicious stubble of new beard. She lifted her head to let him find her throat, his mouth as hungry as his hands, his breath fanning the chills against dampened skin. And when he found her last button, he brushed her blouse off her shoulders, dropping it into a puddle of sunlight on the maroon rug.

His hands swept her arms, spanned her waist, eased up her torso. Cupped her breasts, testing their weight and teasing the nipples to attention without even a touch. Quinn gasped, now furious to feel those fingers against her, her own hands deep inside his shirt, splayed against the crinkle of hair and the thud of his heartbeat.

She was beginning to writhe, her body instinctively joining in the dance, seeking the heat of him even without her permission, her hips easing against his and inviting. His groan was harsh. His reaction was quick. He dropped his hands to her waist and undid her belt, and now his hands were trembling. Quinn smiled, she hummed, deep in her throat, her head back so that she could feel the tumble of hair at her back as he trailed impatient kisses along her throat. Her body was shimmering now, too, pulsating with the music of arousal, coiling tighter and tighter inside her, like a rising wind, a boiling sea, an approaching storm.

She felt his fingers brush the silk at her hips, and her slacks slid down to huddle with her blouse. She stood in flats, bra and panties. And when she stepped out of her shoes, she stood only in her bra and panties. The air swept her. Far outside her open window, she thought the sea was crashing against the rocks. Seabirds cried and the wind answered, and Quinn felt it in her chest. Rising, whirling, keening to be free.

It was her turn. Reaching way up, deliberately stretching up the length of Ian's bare torso with the whisper of lace and silk,

Quinn brushed off his jacket and shirt. She undid his belt and slacks. And finally giving in to an impulse born of a different time, she knelt to kiss the fierce scar at his hip.

It shattered him. Dragging her into his arms, he lifted her onto the bed. Quinn had dreamed of what it would feel like to sink into that soft marshmallow bed alongside him. She'd had no idea. He surrounded her. He consumed her. With his hands and his mouth and his eyes, he worshiped her, stirring that wind in her to a storm that made her whimper and cry. His fingers, those work-roughened fingers that she had so fantasized about, tormented her breasts and her belly and her legs, unleashing chills and sparks that blinded her in the soft shadows of his room. His mouth, so gentle, ravaged her.

And Quinn, suddenly as hungry as he, let her own hands and mouth and body claim him, every inch of muscle and tendon and sinew, so sleek and strong and hard. So rough against the silk of her belly and thighs. He praised her with his touch and she paid him homage with hers. And when he dipped his fingers deep to unleash the heat, she danced with him, sang with him, soared with him. Begged him for release, for union, for completion. She led him to her and guided him home. She wrapped herself around him as he buried himself in her and drank in the sound of her own name on his lips. And when the storm broke over her, she offered his in return, shuddering, sobbing, clutching at him to pull him even closer, closer than possible, because she couldn't get enough of the feel of him in her arms.

He followed her, his voice harsh, his eyes closed, his body filling her with a completion that she'd never known. Quinn held him to her as he relaxed and wondered at the tears that trickled down her cheeks, because she'd never wept in a man's arms before. And when Ian turned and kissed those tears, she smiled and knew she was home.

Ian wasn't sure at first what woke him. He'd fallen asleep on his back, with Quinn nestled against his chest, her hair fanned across his shoulder and her arm thrown over his stomach. The blankets were bunched at their waists, and the sun melted into puddles of rich butter on the floor beyond them.

The daylight was waning, the hours Ian had left to finish his assignment disappearing. Ian couldn't have cared less. For the first time in his life, he felt content. Not just satiated or sleepy or drowsy. Content. Bone-deep satisfaction, as if he'd traveled his entire life just to reach this point. This place, with Quinn asleep in his arms. He couldn't imagine that anything else in the world could feel so good, and he'd experienced quite a bit of the world.

Nothing compared to this, the gentle ebb and flow of her breathing, the spring scent of her hair in his nostrils, the delicious satin of her skin against him. The feeling of utter completion in their lovemaking.

It couldn't last, he knew. He was savoring an island of calm before reality hit again. He was taking advantage of her ignorance. But he couldn't help it. He so feared what he would see in her eyes when she found out just who was about to ask her to marry him that he put it off as long as he could. Because if he saw what he feared, everything that had happened up to this point would be a sham, and he'd have to walk away alone. Again. Always.

Before, he'd tolerated it. He'd almost expected it. Now, he wasn't sure he could bear it.

A chuckle. That's what he'd heard, ethereal and soft, like the fond amusement of a mother at seeing the sillier antics of her children. He heard it again now, hovering somewhere near his door.

Not moving his arm from where it held Quinn close against his chest, Ian looked up into the air with a wry grin. "Think you've got us, do you, you old biddy?"

Quinn stirred against him. "Calling me names already?" she asked, her voice drowsy.

Ian bent to kiss the top of her head, jealously guarding their isolation. "Can't you hear your friend? She thinks this is all pretty funny."

Quinn stretched against him and Ian fought the sudden stab of renewed desire.

"Oh, I'm sure she's seen it all before."

Ian chuckled. "Marvelous. We stumbled upon the only house with a bloody voyeur for a haunt."

Quinn smiled against his chest and snuggled closer, her fingers wandering over his chest. Ian tested the slope of her waist and cupped the swell of her hip with the flat of his hand.

"I saw her, y'know," he admitted, remembering.

Quinn lifted her head. Her hair, deliciously tumbled from their lovemaking, cascaded across her forehead. "You saw who?"

Ian lifted his hand to straighten her hair and spent a few moments wandering himself. "The original leaseholder herself," he said. "Standing over there by the door. She was evidently visiting the sick."

Quinn instinctively looked that way and back again, her eyes wide. "You're sure."

He scowled at her. "As a rule, the only things I hallucinate about when struck with malaria are the dicier moments of my career and racing."

She nodded. "You were trying to get over the fence at Aintree. But you couldn't have seen Mary. Nobody's really *seen* her."

"A rather tall, strong-boned woman," he said. "Margaret Thatcher with a ruff."

Quinn scowled this time. "*I've* never seen her."

Ian couldn't help grinning at her. "You sound jealous."

"Well, my family didn't hang around with Cromwell."

"Not that you know of, at any rate."

She offered a particularly heartfelt grimace. "These are not exactly what you'd call the features of the typical English rose."

No, Ian thought with decided pleasure, they weren't. They were unique, compelling, striking. No one could possibly have the bad taste to mistake this beauty for something as bland as a rose. Taking advantage of the hand still entwined in her hair, Ian pulled her close and took a few minutes delivering his opinion with a silent mouth. She offered up a soft mew of surprise, curled her fingers against his chest, arched against him.

Desire tightened in his belly. He pulled her even closer, suddenly insatiable again. Her breasts were so firm, so soft against him. He sought them out with a hungry hand.

"Alistair will object," she said without much heat, her own hand searching out his arousal.

"Unless His Royal Highness walks through the door this very minute," Ian assured her, "there is nothing more important than what we're doing right now."

Quinn chuckled, bending to nuzzle his ear. Her hair tickled him to distraction. Her hand was working the most delicious magic. "Nothing?" she whispered, shooting chills down the length of his body.

Ian rolled her over and took control of the situation. "Nothing," he assured her, bending to taste her breast. Filling himself with it, with the scent and taste and sound of her as she began that slow undulation beneath him that drove him mad.

"In that case," she gasped, her hands clutching at his back, her legs twining around his, "I guess we'd better... give it our... complete... ooh... attention."

And they did.

The sky was mauve and the ocean silent when they next roused. The house creaked and grumbled around them, and the birds quarreled out beyond the hills. In the distance, cowbells tinkled and a dog barked. The day was easing to a close, a soft English spring day full of promise and birth. A day of future and permanence.

"How *do* you feel about children?" Ian asked, once again holding Quinn close against his chest.

"I told you not to worry," she said.

"Not now," he retorted. "In the near future. To carry on the family name and all that."

She lifted her head, a soft, beguiling expression on her face. "It's not something I've ever really thought much about," she admitted. "I've never really had anything to hand down."

"Of course you do," he argued. "Just because you don't have names to go with those genes doesn't mean they're any less worthy."

She smiled a bit wistfully. "But I don't have any stories to hand down. All my friends heard how their ancestors braved the new world in covered wagons and flatboats and fought brushfires and Indians and draughts. I don't know what my ancestors fought. Where they lived, what traditions were important to them. What they would deem precious enough to hand down to their children, and their children's children."

"Would you settle for handing down mine?"

Quinn went very still against him. Ian held his breath.

"You keep saying things like that," she protested, although she sounded more cautious than upset. "We haven't known each other long enough."

"I think you're wrong," Ian said. "Where I come from people marry who've known each other all their lives, and they end up with pretty boring marriages. They prefer to stick to the certainty, the known factor, and find their fun someplace else. Since I've known you, I've decided I can't live that way. I want my marriage to be the most vital part of my life. I want to share it with the person who means the most to me in the world.''

"And how can you tell after knowing me for so short a time that I'm the one?"

Ian had to smile, hearing his mother's objections just as clearly. "Because the last thing I intended to do on this trip was enjoy myself. And suddenly I'm more alive than I've ever been, and it's all your fault. So, what would you have me do about it?"

"I think you just did," she replied dryly. "Twice."

Ian laughed until his sides ached. "I won't back down," he promised. "I'm going to batter at you until you finally break and admit that what you want most in life is to be married to a broken-down old policeman with a bum leg."

"Whom I still know nothing about," she objected sharply.

Ian raised an eyebrow. "You know I was in the military, I rode horses and I enjoy solving the odd puzzle. I can get you a dinner invite to Kensington Palace and an introduction to some of the better country homes you've always wanted to re-decorate."

"Well, silly me," she retorted. "What more could a girl want to know? I suppose you're happy with my résumé."

Ian pursed his forehead in thought. "There is one thing," he said.

"What, the children?"

"Almost as vital. The horses."

"What about them?"

"Do you ride?"

Quinn's smile was terribly smug. "Are you ready to go downstairs?" she asked. "Because I'd like to show you some-thing."

Ian thought about it for a moment. "My stomach is growl-ing," he admitted.

Dressing seemed to entail a lot of laughter, not all of it be-yond the earthly plane. When clothes were right side out and sufficiently neat, Quinn led Ian out the door and across the hall to her room.

Ian hadn't noticed the grouping of framed pictures on her bedside table. Children, adults, gatherings. Quinn picked up one in particular and showed it to him.

"My sister and I," she said.

Two girls at the braces-and-pigtails age, polar in appearance, one slim and dark in her Stetson and jeans, the other similarly dressed but chubby and blond. Both seated astride what appeared to be well-bred quarter horses. Both displaying trophies and excited, shy smiles.

Ian looked up accusingly. "You competed?"

"Junior champion from Iowa," she said with a grin. "The American version of the steeplechase. Rodeo. I was a barrel racer."

Ian looked back at the picture, at the easy way Quinn sat the horse, the pride and achievement in those young brown eyes. An emotion he remembered too well.

"Not much call for that in Europe, I imagine," he said, amazed.

"Not since Wild Bill Hickock went home," she agreed. "It's an added bonus at some of the places I've worked. I get free access to the stables."

Ian looked up in surprise. "Then why haven't you given Blackie a run for his money?"

"Are you kidding?" She returned the picture to the table. "I'm adventuresome. Not suicidal. I'm still trying to figure out how you ever even got on that beast in the first place, much less completed an entire race on him."

"Oh, he's not so bad."

"He's put three stable boys in the hospital since he's been here."

Ian chuckled. "Then I'll just have to show you amateurs how it's done."

Quinn turned to follow Ian toward the stairs. "Not on my account, thanks."

He couldn't say why. Maybe the fact that he was still flushed with exhilaration. Maybe the sense of adventure Quinn woke once again in him. For some reason, Ian suddenly wanted to be down at those stables.

His heels echoed from the wooden staircase as they descended. "Come on, yank. It's easy."

Quinn turned on him, halfway down, and stopped. "You're serious. Ian, don't do something silly. You're only just starting to feel better. You just had your leg worked on."

Ian scowled at her and grabbed her hand. "And I'm feeling just a bit frisky. Come along."

"Ah, there you two are," Alistair announced, stepping from the salon where he'd obviously been waiting impatiently. The base of his neck was almost purple with discomfort. "I, um, resettled the library, of course. Ingenious of the old girl, don't you think?"

"You're a cavalry man," Ian said instead of answering. "Don't you think it's high time we showed that horse out there who's in charge?"

Completely confused now, Alistair looked out toward the stables, then at Ian, then at Quinn.

"He's gone mad." She shrugged. "He's decided he wants to ride Blackie."

"But no one's actually ridden the beast since he's been here. He keeps biting everyone, don't you see."

Ian laughed. "Not you, too, Colonel. Well, I can see this is something I'll have to do alone."

He didn't, of course. Quinn and Alistair followed him out into the evening. Ian couldn't account for his sudden madness. He hadn't done anything like this since his days in the SAS, when it had been positively encouraged. Mountain climbing, free-falling, climbing out a train window onto the roof at sixty miles an hour just to see how long it would take to walk from one end of the train to the other.

Blackie wasn't in the same league, of course. No matter how the old rogue had fared, Ian knew his tricks. But suddenly Ian wanted to shatter the schedule. He wanted to do something just for the hell of it.

The stables were part of the Victorian addition, brick and solid, each box opening into the yard. Blackie was in the far box. Hearing the approaching feet, he leaned his head out the open door and whinnied.

"Well, there you are, you old sod," Ian snarled at him, knowing just what the horse would do. The animal gave the box a great kick and whinnied again, his way of saying hello.

Ian walked right up to the box and threw open the door. He heard the colonel beat a strategic retreat. Quinn held her ground, which made Ian smile.

"Well, then," he challenged the horse. "It's time for a run, isn't it? Get up here, you great packet of dog food."

Blackie gingerly stepped out into the gravel yard. Not backing up an inch, Ian reached up and grabbed him by the halter. Blackie shied. Ian gave the halter a good yank and pulled the horse's face right down alongside his. Ian stared in Blackie's left eye. Never said a word. Just stared, the same way he used to at new recruits the military was trying to weed out.

Blackie didn't utter a sound. Quinn and the colonel stood by. Ian counted to thirty and then walked around and grabbed a handful of mane and hoisted himself onto Blackie's back. Blackie took a couple of steps, but otherwise held perfectly still.

"Good heavens . . ." the colonel breathed in amazement.

"Not just yet," Ian cautioned, consolidating his grip. "Back up a little."

They did, just in time. With one great snort, Blackie reared up on his hind legs with every intention of scraping Ian off against the stable door. Ian laughed.

And that was it. Blackie settled back onto the regulation four legs and stood there, tail swishing and ears forward.

Lifting a hand in salute, Ian looked down for Quinn's judgment. "See?" he asked. "Even old has-beens can still answer the call to arms if need be. What do you think?"

She tilted her head, with that smile that said so much. "About what?" she asked. "The horse, the children?"

He smiled back, completely satisfied. "The policeman."

She seemed to be considering it. The colonel interrupted her.

"Oh, my God!" he gasped suddenly, his great mustache bristling. "Giggleswick!"

Quinn turned to the colonel and back to where the horse still stood placidly with Ian in the saddle. "Giggleswick? Where? I thought he was dead."

"He was," the colonel muttered, shaking his head.

"Oh, great," Quinn mourned. "Another ghost. Just when I was beginning to get a handle on one."

"Not that Giggleswick," Alistair protested, and Ian knew he was sunk. The old man threw an accusing hand in his direction and blustered all over again. "*That* Giggleswick!"

Still Quinn didn't follow. "Where?"

Smythe-Smithe looked at her as if she were not only backward, but stubborn, as well. "When Nigel, the Viscount Gig-

gleswick died, his brother Ian naturally assumed the title,'' he
said, and then turned astonished eyes on Ian. "My God, man,
why didn't you tell us you were the heir to the Earldom of
Malham?''

Eleven

Here it comes, Ian thought with desperation. The sudden light in her eyes, the complacent assurance, the avarice.

"A viscount?" she'd say. "The Earl of Malham? Oh, yes, Ian, of course I'll be your wife." She'd be a countess. A *rich* countess. He'd already run from at least two dozen prospective brides simply because he'd seen that in their eyes, the attraction to the title instead of the man. Once they heard the word "earl," the Christian name was interchangeable. Could he really hope that Quinn would be all that different?

His chest already on fire, even before Quinn recovered from her frozen posture of astonishment, Ian swung down off Blackie and backed him into the box to give each of them a little time.

"We'll have a ride later," he promised the gelding, shutting and latching the door. He didn't even feel the sharp teeth skim the top of his head.

"Excuse me, my lord," the colonel blustered, suddenly furiously embarrassed at his casual address. "I didn't actually mean to... *chastise* you, don't you know."

Ian wanted to wince all over again. The distance was suddenly there, the formality, the expectations.

Bracing against the inevitable sight of Quinn's new interest, Ian slapped the old man on the arm. "I do a much more efficient job if people simply don't know," he said. "I prefer first names, if you don't mind."

"It was the horse, of course. Should have recognized you sooner, but the minute I saw you up there I remembered the Gold Cup. Smashing ride, what? Quite a career you've had, sir. Military Cross and all, and still competing. I can remember the news accounts as if they were yesterday. Should have spotted you right away, of course, but there it is. Didn't expect you here, and all that."

Ian barely heard him. He'd walked over to where Quinn stood, her head down, her jaw working, her hands shoved into her pants pockets.

"Well?" he asked, his voice unconsciously challenging. "Are you still interested?"

"An earl?" she asked without looking up. "You're really going to be an earl?"

"If I don't precede my dear pater," he drawled, steeling himself. "But of course, Mama wants me to marry as soon as possible, since if I don't provide issue, the dreaded cousin Gervase the Sot gets his incapable hands on the whole lot."

"Well, we can't have that," she countered, and Ian's hopes fell further.

Here it comes.

"No," he agreed. "We can't. What do you say?"

"To marrying you?" she countered. Then she lifted her head and Ian saw the look in her eyes. "No way, bud."

Ian's mouth gaped in a most ungentlemanly fashion. Alistair made apoplectic noises. Quinn whirled on her heel before either of them could catch her and stalked back to the house.

"What do you mean, no way?" Ian demanded, slamming in the house behind her.

Quinn didn't bother to turn around. She was seething, the fury close enough to threaten tears. She didn't need to face him, because it would weaken her case. She didn't need to battle him like a harpy. She just needed to figure out how the hell she was going to get away.

So far she wasn't having any luck. Ian caught up with her dead center in the foyer and grabbed her by the arm. "I said," he repeated, his voice like steel as he whirled her around to face him. "What do you mean?"

She challenged him, his handsome face blurring just a little as she fought for control. "I said no. Period. End of discussion. Now, if you don't mind, I have other things to do."

Ian seemed completely nonplussed by her answer. Quinn turned away and kept walking. He followed along right behind her.

"There's something wrong with marrying me now that you know who I am?"

She spun on him, too much boiling in her to get out. "First of all," she snapped, jabbing him in his perfectly tailored, crisp cotton shirt, "there's the matter of telling me a whole host of lies about just who you were."

"But I *am* a policeman," he protested, arms out. "Ask my superiors. Ask the Queen if you want!"

Quinn kept jabbing. "And then there's the overwhelming suspicion I have that old Giggleswick—" her face squinched up as if she'd just caught an unpleasant smell "—is that *really* your name?"

Ian instinctively straightened, as if she'd insulted his legitimacy. "It's a beautiful little village in Yorkshire," he informed her archly. "The site of the early Spears-Wykeham holdings."

"Oh," she countered, hands now on hips. "Is that the name now? Not Matthews, but Spears-Wykeham? With a hyphen?"

"Something wrong with hyphens?" he demanded.

"They're pretentious," she snapped. "And just who the hell *is* Matthews?"

"My mother's family," he said. "I use it when I'm undercover."

"What about Ian?" she demanded. "Who's he, the butler?"

"My name," he grated, "is Ian Matthew George Elliott Spears-Wykeham."

"The Viscount Giggleswick."

"Yes."

Quinn huffed at him, all the new information piling inexorably toward disaster. Burying her beneath the certainty that she'd just made the same mistake she'd made five years ago. It infuriated her.

"I have the feeling," she said dryly, "that old Ian Matthew George Elliott Spears-Wykeham, the Viscount Giggleswick, has spent his time here in Cornwall slumming. Mingling with the little people. Seeing how the other half lives."

She could see the barb hit its mark. Ian flushed and straightened even more, making her wonder if he was going to snap like a branch in a high wind.

"Well, I'm not playing, buddy," she snapped, her finger once again hitting its target just to the left of his third button. "I'm not going to do the first act of 'Cinderella' just because you think it might be fun to throw a little time away on one of the peasant girls. Somebody Mummy would never approve of, someone salacious and forbidden, just to stir things up back at the country house."

She was all set to turn away when the thought hit her, the latest in a long list of betrayals. "My God," she snarled, whirling back on him before he got a chance to argue. "You didn't just *visit* Malham Hall. You grew up there. You had a Rembrandt in your television room and a Hobart over the breakfast table. You son of a bitch."

And then she got away before he could stop her again.

"Brilliant performance," the colonel whispered in Ian's ear. "That should have the old girl spinning, what?"

Ian gave a start. He'd been standing there watching the empty stairs Quinn had just climbed.

No. She'd said no. And she'd said it in no uncertain terms. It hadn't been certainty he'd discovered in her features, or smug assurance. It had been fury. Blind, black rage. Betrayal. She'd accused him of everything from collusion to pandering, and then she'd stomped off.

Now what the hell was he supposed to do?

"I need to talk to her," Ian protested, almost to himself. "She has to understand."

"Oh, no, sir," Alistair protested. "Not just yet. Besides, won't it be much more...advantageous in the old dining room this evening?"

Ian spun on the old man, irritated and sharp, and then saw that the colonel had no idea what was bothering Ian so much.

"Quite," Ian agreed with a small smile as he fought for control. "Now, if you don't mind, I have some work to do."

"Of course, my lord."

"And Colonel," he cautioned. "I'm still undercover. Please remember to refer to me by my given name."

The old man lifted a finger to the side of his nose and nodded. "Good show, sir."

Ian gave up with a sigh and headed up the stairs.

Damn it. Damn it. Damn it. Quinn paced her room, threw pillows at the bed, opened her windows, thought about escaping and then decided she'd be damned if she was going to let Ian chase her off.

The Earl of Malham. One of the last real seats of power in the English peerage, the various family members counseling kings and queens all the way back to Bosworth Field. The present earl sat in the House of Lords, of course, when he wasn't busy at the odd grouse shoot or Jockey Club benefit. Not just rich, but obscenely rich, skirting the tax man with a century of sharp businessmen and fresh capital from smart marriages and mergers. The epitome of the country gentleman, snowy-white hair and courtly manners, with just the slightest aftertaste of disdain in his manner.

Legendary family, legendary wealth, customs and dictates that stretched back into the dim origins of English history. The quintessential British peerage.

Jason Aubuchon with an attitude. Oh, God, how did she let herself get into these situations? It wasn't just that Ian's family would definitely and vocally not approve of her, it was that once married, it would naturally be expected that in exchange for the privilege of carrying the valued family name, she would of course uphold the valued family standards.

And if there was one thing Quinn had learned in her disastrous attempt at marriage, that sort of thing wasn't something anyone should demand of her. She had tried her best, letting her own needs and goals disappear beneath the weight of all those upper-scale expectations. She'd let her mind fade into vague blandness, because the most it had been needed for was scheduling and manners and the very precise art of whom not to sit next to whom at a dinner party because the one was the other's husband's mistress.

Damn it. And she'd actually been coveting a house of her own. A family to come home to. A tradition of her own to begin.

In retribution, she called Allison.

"Why the hell didn't you tell me?" she demanded without even benefit of a greeting.

There were sounds of a party in the background, glassware and cutlery tinkling, laughter. Allison was famous for her parties. The minute she heard the tone of Quinn's voice, her ladyship closed a door to cut off the noise and company and paid attention.

"What's wrong, Quinn?"

"You didn't tell me. *Nobody* told me who he was!"

"But he was undercover. I thought that was the whole idea."

Quinn threw herself flat on the bed and covered her eyes with an arm. "Not when I'm falling in love with him, it isn't!"

Allison's knowing chuckle should have incensed her. Instead it made her want to weep.

"And what's wrong with that? Once in the distant past I cast my own considerable attentions Ian's way. Before I met Charlie, of course."

"That's different," Quinn protested, wishing desperately that her body still didn't vaguely ache from the delicious afternoon she'd spent. If only it hadn't felt so wonderful. If only she hadn't felt such a sense of homecoming in his arms.

"What's different?" Allison demanded. "Are you saying he's too good for you?"

"I'm saying I'm too good for him."

There was another chuckle, this time dryer. "Oh, my dear, you can be such a snob."

Quinn couldn't help grinning, even through the tears that now trickled into her ears. "And don't ever forget it," she challenged, her voice breaking miserably. "I thought he was a policeman."

"Oh, he is," Allison assured her. "Drives his dear *maman* the countess mad. The whole family was incensed enough when he transferred from the venerable Guards into the very plebeian SAS. Then to retire into the London police force was almost too much for them. Especially when he rather abruptly became the viscount. If an earl must make a living, they'd much rather he be a photog or something, don't you know."

"The Guards," Quinn echoed. "Not the Greens. I should have known."

"No other branch of the service, my dear," her friend drawled. "We nasty brood of inheritors may give lip service to equality and progressive thinking, darling, but we don't really mean it. Not in our heart of hearts."

"And certainly not *that* family."

Allison's laugh was one of pure delight. "They feel they've single-handedly kept the light of civilization lit in the wilds of the Yorkshire moors for centuries." There was a brief pause. "Are you truly saying you don't want the chance at having Malham Hall all for yourself?"

Quinn fought new, hotter tears. "Just because a prison is beautiful doesn't mean the bars on the windows aren't as strong."

"Ouch. You really are quite unique. Ian had better snatch you up while he has the chance."

"Ian is not going to 'snatch me up,'" Quinn said haughtily. "I have no intention of reliving the most claustrophobic marriage of the twentieth century, thank you very much."

Another pause, the famous English search for discretion. "I don't think you're quite giving Ian a chance," Allison said carefully. "Try to do so before you chuck him out."

"How can I chuck him out?" Quinn demanded miserably. "He owns the place."

The colonel didn't get his wish. There was no meal served in the dining room that evening. Quinn never emerged from her room, and Ian settled for munching on a couple of apples and a tin of salmon alone in the gleaming, echoing kitchen. He shivered in the damp chill of the great house, listening for life inside it, straining to hear Quinn returning, and heard only the soft mutterings of an old building. The kind of company he'd always had growing up as a child.

No parents about. Nanny, with her stern mouth and brisk no-nonsense manner, ruling her domain with a command such as Ian had never seen in his years in the service. Still a substitute for parents who seemed only to vaguely remember they had more than one child, the child born and groomed to be the next earl, the one upon which ancient aspirations hung, upon which every burden and benefit of the estates and various business and real-estate ventures would fall. Nigel, called to account, constantly reminded of his position, his potential, his place. Distant, older, silent Nigel who'd matured not into a gentleman, but a selfish eccentric without real mourners at his funeral.

And then Ian and Beatrice, the also-rans, brought into the world simply in the event that anything went wrong with Nigel. Well, something had gone wrong, but by then Ian had been too long forgotten, too well versed in his role as second son, as standby, to really appreciate his good fortune.

By then he'd set out on his own course, as other second sons had before him, in an occupation safe for a second son, with enough money to sustain the life, enough prestige to sustain the family name, enough exposure to ensure the family line.

He hadn't realized how far he'd strayed from the Malham priorities until the moment Quinn had turned him down. He'd always thought he'd objected to his mother's efforts solely on the basis of principle. He'd find his own wife, thank you. One who at least suited him better than the dreaded Gwendolyn, who seemed to come with the package when Nigel had had the bad grace to die. Now, suddenly, the thought of losing Quinn's special spark, her wit, her intelligence, her unique life, shattered him.

It wasn't simply that he'd wanted to stake his own course. He'd known from the moment Nigel had hit that hill in Switzerland that his life would change. It was just a question of how much. With Quinn he'd have had a chance to hold on to as much of himself as he needed. With Quinn he wouldn't have disappeared into the title the way his father, and his father before him, had. He would have been able to remain the man his maternal grandfather was, a rogue who had chosen his bride because she'd been the only woman with nerve enough to argue with him, the Duke of Winston.

She'd become the Duchess of Winston, that sharp, knowing, formidable woman. But more than that, she'd been his wife, his partner, his love. Ian had spent summers at his grandmother's and learned that lesson at her knee. And now, he wanted to carry it on. He wanted Quinn to save him from what he could become.

First thing in the morning, he went to tell her that. He found her in the great hall, a snifter of cognac in her hand.

"A little early for that, isn't it?" he asked.

The sun shafted in from the high windows, milky with morning light, and warmed her hair to a fine umber. She was pacing, her usual slacks and blouse replaced by a sweater and an ice-white jersey dress that swirled softly around lithe legs.

Looking at her, Ian couldn't believe she hadn't slept the entire night. She looked soft and vulnerable, her eyes huge, her movements brisk and businesslike. He'd heard her tossing and turning across the hall. He'd heard her because he'd been tossing right along with her.

"It's cold in here," she said, sipping at the golden liquid.

Ian tested the air and nodded. A definite chill in the atmosphere, the damp of night resisting eviction from the hall's heavy stone.

"In that case," he said, "we'll light a fire."

The room was wood floored, with half a dozen faded Oriental carpets to cover it, several groupings of comfortable couches and chairs, so that a good twenty or so people could chat in the room without interfering with one another. Considering the fact that this high, echoing room had once held great banquets with hundreds of guests and the necessary staff, the effect Quinn had struck with the decor was surprisingly intimate.

"And pour me one, too," he said on his way by her.

"Would my lord like brandy or cognac?" she retorted sharply.

Ian turned on her. "Stop it, Quinn. I couldn't tell anyone who I was. After seeing how the colonel reacted, surely you can see why."

"Of course I can," she conceded, her voice still as stiff and unyielding as ever. "What kind of fun would that be? Now you'll have just scads of *riveting, brilliant* stories to tell all your friends at the next hunt." Her eyes glittered, hard and hurt beyond Ian's understanding. Far beyond the shallow barbs of her words.

"I already told you," he said, fighting to keep his hands to himself, desperate to have her back in his arms, "I had no intentions of falling in love when I got here. I had a job to do, and that was part of it."

"And when were you going to tell me?" she demanded. "When we were on the way to meet mums? On the way to the altar? 'Oh, by the way, Quinn, darling, I'm not quite the son of a vicar. Me old man's an earl, so he is. Richest bleeding sod south of the Queen herself. You don't mind, do you?' "

"Why do you?" he retorted. "You didn't exactly find out that I've been chopping shop girls into bits and floating them down the Thames."

"Maybe that would have been easier," she snapped. "At least I'd know you weren't laughing at me."

"Laughing?"

"I say, my . . . er, Ian." Alistair stood in the doorway, stiff with discomfort, bristling with urgency. "There's a phone call for you. Sir Basil again. Seems they have a spot more trouble."

Ian didn't move. For a long moment he couldn't even pull his gaze from Quinn's. The air shuddered between them, suddenly close and brittle.

"I'll be right back," he promised, then turned to the colonel. "And don't let her out of here." He heard Quinn sputter behind him, but Ian was already through the door and on his way down the hall.

Damn her. How could she believe he'd been laughing at her? How could she possibly think that what had happened between them had been anything but magical? What was suddenly so wrong with him that she should look at him as if he'd crawled out from beneath a rock?

"Yes, Sir Basil," he said, picking up the phone.

"How are things coming along, then, Ian?"

It took Ian a millisecond to comprehend, another to shift mental gears. "Your office should have received the diagrams yesterday," he said, dropping back into the desk chair. "At present I'm still working on layouts. The foreign office was quite correct—there's plenty of room here, isolation and protection. I've been in the village, and we can expect all the help and discretion we need from them."

"Ah, good. Good. Brilliant job, as usual."

"How is His Royal Highness's trip to the riot areas going?" he asked.

"So far no incidents. Wembley might just make a decent replacement if you should decide to decamp at any point."

Ian scowled. This was not the moment he wanted to hear that he was superfluous. "And the threatening letters?"

"Ah, yes. Those. Bit of a problem there, I'm afraid. Word's leaked that the king and the sheik are meeting here. There've been protests and counterprotests all along embassy row."

Ian leaned his head on his hands and fought the urge to groan. "Any indication that the actual site has been discovered?"

"Not so far. Although our friends have contacted us again— amid all the other threatening mail, of course."

"What do they say?"

"More about prisoners, rights—although there seems to be something about children in this latest communiqué. They mention 'the helpless small creatures.'"

"Either children or jockeys," Ian muttered dryly.

"Yes, well, these particular victims seem to be imprisoned. We still haven't a clue as to which head of state is holding them, though. You'd think this bunch would at least be good enough to specify."

"Especially if they're planning on blowing up whoever it is," Ian agreed.

"Um, there is one more thing," Sir Farquhar said. "They know our timetable."

Ian's head snapped up. "They what?"

"The note mentions dates. The new dates. To be perfectly frank, Ian, it concerns me. They speak of a preemptive strike, a warning-off, so to speak. It says, 'We will show our complete commitment. Hopefully this will convince Your Highness that we are willing to sacrifice everything for the sake of the small helpless ones.'"

"Odd," Ian muttered.

"Quite."

"Any information on atrocities against children on either side?"

"Not that we can find. We've had people poring through every source we can. There is quite a bit of starvation in Barouet, but that seems more the sudden draught than the sheik's whims."

"A preemptive strike," Ian echoed softly, rubbing his forehead. He didn't like the sound of that at all. It almost sounded as if the terrorists were letting them know that they had found the site. They had the new updated schedule. They spoke of jumping in first. They might just try something in the next few days.

He had to get Quinn out of Hartley Hall.

Quinn should have been finishing up her work on the communion rail. She should have been on the phone following up on the linen order that was due in day after tomorrow. She should have been making sure that the kitchens were going to work for the staff who would be accompanying the conference attendees.

Instead she sat in the overstuffed chair in front of the cold empty fireplace in the great hall and thought about the future. The kind she wanted and the kind she'd never have. The kind other people expected. The kind Ian was offering.

She took another sip of cognac and realized the snifter was empty. Her belly was warm. Her lips were a little numb. She hadn't had breakfast or dinner the night before, and the cognac had settled on her like a comfortable mist. Carefully climbing to her feet, Quinn went in search of just a little more. Just enough to make her really warm, when no matter what she wore or how many covers she piled on her during the night, she still felt deathly, fatally cold. Unwarmable. Unbearable.

The cognac splashed into the balloon-shaped glass and swirled in a golden whirlpool. Quinn grinned a bit lopsidedly at it. She didn't even like cognac that much. She preferred a sweeter drink, something innocuous and easy to hold all evening during a party as she watched everyone else get progressively looser. Somehow, though, the cognac was just what she needed right now. Pungent, strong, searing.

She'd already settled back into the chair when she heard a familiar uneven stride approaching down the hallway. She lifted the glass and took another good slug, telling herself that her eyes were only watering from the liquor.

"Quinn?"

His voice was a bark of command. Quinn winced at the sound as it echoed off the high stone walls. Instead of answering, she closed her eyes. If she just ignored him, maybe he'd go away.

She heard a soft curse and thought she'd actually won. But instead of receding back down the hall toward the front rooms, the sound of footfalls approached, a syncopation of authority, control.

"Answer me, damn it," he snapped, stopping right before her chair.

Quinn opened one eye and scowled at him. "Is this the next step after flattery and bribery?"

He stared hard at her. "How many glasses of that have you had?"

Quinn looked down at her nearly empty glass. "I don't know. A few."

"Good God, Quinn," he railed. "It's only eleven in the morning."

"Like they say," she retorted, finishing off the liquid in a manner that would have had cognac connoisseurs the world over wincing. "Somewhere in the world it's after five."

Ian didn't answer her. He seemed to be holding counsel with himself, hands on hips, weight on his good leg, head down. "We need to talk," he said. "Now." Without waiting for a response, he pulled another chair closer to her and sat down.

"We've talked," she said with a shake of her head, struggling to get back to her feet.

Ian gave her an unceremonious little push on the chest that sent her right back into her chair.

"Sit," he commanded.

She glared at him. "That's abuse," she snarled. "I'm not going to have you shoving me around."

"Quinn," he said, his face a study in patience, "I don't have time to be polite. You have to listen to me, and I don't have time to wait around for you to make up your mind to do it."

She lifted her glass. "At least freshen my drink."

"No."

"I'm cold."

"I'll build a fire," he countered. "In a minute."

She glared at him. "If I'm going to be forced to sit and listen to you recite your pedigree, the least you could do is build me a fire now."

Ian took a moment to consult with some inner voice. Then, with a shake of his head, he pushed himself to his feet and stalked over to the huge expanse of deep echoing shadow that was the great-hall fireplace. A man could easily stand inside. The mantel, now perfectly refitted, was granite with the Trewelyn family crest carved over the center and a brace of stags holding up the corners. Dead center in the block or so of smoke-blackened flooring were piled several huge logs that could have each floated a dozen people. Alistair had built the fire the night before, leaving nothing to do but sprinkle on the kindling and touch the flame.

Ian bent to place the kindling. Quinn couldn't take her eyes from the way his flannel slacks lay over his backside and legs. Taut sleek lines. Rock-solid muscle sliced by whipcord tendons. Tears stung her eyes again at the memory of the feel of them in her hands. The smell of him, the taste of him.

"And after I lay the bloody fire," he snapped, his voice a hollow echo up the vast chimney, "you're going to sit there and damn well listen to what I have to say."

Quinn heard the sudden shriek of metal. She saw Ian lift his head, his mouth open in surprise. She had too much alcohol on board to do more than open her own mouth, dismally short of warning, caught short of astonishment.

Before either of them could do more than gape, the chimney flue clanged and half a ton of soot cascaded onto Ian's upturned face.

Twelve

Quinn did a very foolish thing. She burst out laughing. In fact, she dropped her glass on the floor and clutched her sides, the sight of Ian's astonished eyes peering out through all that black sending her into fresh paroxysms. He was covered head to toe with the stuff, his hands out as if in supplication, his eyes a circle of shocking white, his mouth clenched shut in fury.

And that was before Mary joined in the laughter.

"Oh, I say," Alistair greeted them from the doorway. "Smashing. How did you find that one?"

Quinn started laughing all over again.

"If you wouldn't mind, **old** man," Ian grated, raising a small cloud of dust around him, "I'd appreciate a dressing gown."

"Of course," Alistair said, running off to help.

Ian stepped off the hearth and Quinn lifted a hand in warning. "Don't track that stuff all over my house," she warned.

Ian glared at her. She laughed some more.

Moving very carefully, he pulled off his shoes and socks, then slid out of his blackened jacket. All of these were set carefully on the fireplace tile. Finally giving in to good grace and sense, Quinn climbed out of her chair to help. By the time

Quinn walked back into the hall with a bag for Ian's clothes, he was standing in just his shorts, looking very much like a chimney sweep after a hard day.

Quinn suppressed another giggle. It would have been a lot funnier if it didn't hurt so much to realize she probably would have been happier if he'd really been a chimney sweep.

"Here," she said, handing him the robe Alistair had provided. "Why don't you go on up and bathe. I'll get these cleaned in town for you." She lifted wry eyes his way and tilted her head. "Who do I bill for it, exactly? The Queen? The Prince?"

"Heritage House," he retorted irritably, slipping into the robe and belting it. Quinn knew then that he really was an upper-class Englishman, because no other species of animal on earth could have made his exit from that room with nearly as much aplomb. She just shook her head and lifted her eyes to the ethereal plane.

"You and I have to talk, Mary," she warned. "This really can't go on."

Her answer for now was another rumble of laughter.

"You're right, though," Quinn agreed, carefully folding the bag over the ruined clothes. "It was pretty funny."

His hair was still a bit damp, curling back by his ears. Quinn couldn't take her eyes off it. He'd changed into corduroy slacks and a knit sweater, the most casual attire she'd ever seen him in. It was even more becoming than the razor-sharp tailoring of the pinstripes and tweeds.

He caught up with her out along the front drive where the oaks muttered with the wind and the neighbor's sheep trimmed the lawn. A bucolic day with fluffy white clouds and crisp blue sky. Alive with the scents of spring, the music of the country. Quinn kicked at the gravel along the drive and kept her head down.

"I'm sorry," she said even before he got the chance to greet her.

That seemed to bring him up a bit short. "For what?" he asked.

She shot him a sideways glance. "I shouldn't have laughed. I shouldn't have had three glasses of cognac instead of cereal for breakfast. I shouldn't have been such a pig this morning.

I'm not really a pleasant person if I haven't had any sleep the night before.''

He nodded, slid into step with her and walked on out toward the distant gate where he'd blown a tire so long ago. "Does this mean you'll listen to what I have to say and be reasonable about it?''

She looked at him. "Depends on what you have to say.''

They stopped together, the shade of new leaves dappling them, the breeze stirring their hair, the sun warming their faces. So close and yet carefully apart. Back to strangers, hesitant acquaintances, nervously testing new waters.

"I need your help," he said simply, and Quinn was surprised. No, stunned. She'd really thought he was going to head back into the subject of marriage. Of the earldom and all its joys.

"Your help?" she echoed. "Of course. What can I do?''

There was a brief flash of a smile, a grudging ruefulness, as if Ian, too, were thinking of a completely different subject than the one he broached.

Even so, he lifted his head, stuffed his hands in his pants pockets and faced her with his request. "I'm afraid there's been a change in the situation regarding the conference. We may not have as much time as we thought to get things settled.''

Quinn immediately stiffened. "Oh, hell. They're coming sooner?" She automatically turned back toward the house. "I'm not ready yet.''

Ian's hands came out and stopped her where she was.

"No," he said with a shake of his head, turning her back to face him. "Not the conference itself. Just the preparations. I want you out of the hall within the next few days.''

"Out?" She looked up at the concern in his eyes and faltered, suddenly uncertain. "But I'm still the one in charge. I can't just walk out of there.''

"The colonel can handle things.''

Quinn's laugh was abrupt. "The colonel is a wonderful manager," she agreed. "He'll be fine once everything is in place and functioning. He has no idea of what instructions to give the artisans, though. He wouldn't know a cabbage rose from a cabbage worm. And if you're bringing in all that electronic equipment, I have to make sure it's not going to overload any circuits or damage any of the furnishings. All those military men in their hobnail boots over my refinished flooring, helicopters scaring the sheep—"

Ian gave her a little shake. "Quinn. Those things don't matter. Not against your safety."

She blinked up at him. "Ian, what are you talking about?"

"I have a bad feeling," he admitted. "This situation is volatile enough with all the secrecy in place. But now word has leaked out that the talks are going to be held in Britain, and every fanatic on three continents has been heard from. I don't want to risk the chance that they know where the conference is going to be held."

Her heart thudded, dropping like a rock. "You really think the hall's in jeopardy, don't you?"

Ian didn't insult her by denying it. "I can take care of things at the hall," he told her. "It's you I'm worried about."

Quinn stole a look back at the house, where it rose in perfect proportion from the lawn, gray stone and glittering glass, a forest of chimneys, the great arch of the front doorway.

She thought of her first sight of the place, crumbling, forgotten, given over to the birds and the bats, with Mary's stubborn voice the only thing but for the cobwebs to fill the half-ruined rooms. She thought of the planning, the designing, the little bits of that house she'd crafted by hand.

"I don't have to go far," she countered, turning pleading eyes back on Ian. "Do I?"

"Would you like to stay in the village?" he asked. "Just until I'm satisfied it's safe?"

She nodded, torn, confused, anxious. Needing to say more to Ian and not knowing what.

"You're going to need to prioritize the work that has to be done before the delegates arrive, and see that it's done. I can get some crews from the army in."

"Engineers hanging wallpaper?" she demanded with a grin. "That I'd almost like to see."

"We also need to figure out some way to defuse that ghost."

Quinn looked again at the house. "I can't imagine she could possibly have any more traps set in there. I think she's just used up the lot on you."

"Traps aren't the only problem," Ian said wryly.

Quinn nodded thoughtfully. "We have to appeal to her altruistic side."

She was surprised by Ian's bark of laughter. "Altruistic? Quinn, I'm afraid you're thinking of the wrong ghost. That old biddy in there doesn't have an altruistic bone in her body— figuratively speaking, of course."

"Sure she does," Quinn objected. "Some things matter very much to her." Then Quinn gave way to a grin. "You just don't seem to be one of them."

Ian scowled at her, hands back in his pockets, as they stood watching the harmless-looking house.

"What, then?" he asked.

"The animals," she answered immediately. "She never hurt Copenhagen. In fact, she hums to him. He kind of likes it."

Ian's head swung around. "Hums?"

"You've heard it, too? For some reason the last week or so, she's been very fond of 'Greensleeves.' I have to admit that's not one I've heard before."

Ian didn't seem particularly enchanted by the news. "What else?"

"'Barbara Allen.' She really likes that one."

"No, I mean, what other things matter to her?"

"Her house, of course. I think she's been really pleased with the renovations, especially the chapel. I walked in one morning to find a rose in there, as white as the snow, right on top of the altar."

"What makes you think she was the one to put it there?"

"It was the middle of January. And Gwynnup Green doesn't have a florist that specializes in floribundas. Anyway, she's fought everybody who's come along and tried to hurt her house. She's also very fond of the village, of course."

Ian turned on her with that, his eyes lighting. "Does she listen to you?"

"She doesn't listen to *anybody* unless it suits her."

"But if you explained to her that sabotaging the conference could hurt not only the village but the hall itself, she might just pay attention."

"And she might not. It's worth a try, though." Quinn thought about it briefly, then nodded. "Heck, anything's worth a try. What's the worst thing she can do to me?"

"I wouldn't ask," Ian suggested dryly. "At least, not if you're standing anywhere near the fireplace at the time."

Quinn chuckled and thought how comfortable it could be with Ian, how in a matter of only days they'd found each other's rhythms, their instinctive comforts. It seemed suddenly as if she'd always looked up to find him standing there before her, his handsome face angled in the sunlight, his eyes soft and tender, his attention all hers.

Damn it. Why did he have to be a viscount?

"Want to go try now?" she asked, dropping her gaze to the gravel and digging at it with her toe. The wind was swirling her skirt and chilling her legs. She barely noticed. She felt only the heat of Ian's gaze on the top of her head.

"How could you think I'd laugh at you?" he asked abruptly.

Her head came up. He was sincere, a raw pain in his eyes, a surprising uncertainty in his stance.

"Ian," she protested, her voice small, "we have a ghost to worry about. Terrorists cresting the hill. Don't you think this should wait a little while?"

"No. I have to understand what's suddenly wrong between us."

She couldn't stop a small laugh of disbelief. "What's wrong is that I should have known better. I should have realized that no policeman would have ridden a prize steeplechaser. No policeman would have been on Best Mess Buddy terms with a prince. No second-son-of-a-vicar policeman could have instructed me quite so succinctly about just how a proper country house should look."

"I told you," he insisted, "I *am* a policeman. I worked my way up from constable to inspector, just like everyone else in the CID. And then I was asked if I'd like to volunteer for the Royal Protection Department for a few years. I enjoy what I do. I'm a very good policeman, and a better detective. Tell me what's wrong with that."

"What's wrong with that is that you're also the heir to one of the largest estates in the British Isles. Do you really think you're going to be able to just stay one of the guys on the force when you're Lord Malham? I know exactly what's going to happen. You're going to give up the force for the House of Lords. You're going to weekend up at Malham Hall and ride to the hounds when it suits you and have little Ians and Nigels to carry on the family name. You're going to be ever so proper and marry a girl who can be ever so proper with you. And that's not me."

"You keep saying that. How do you know what I'll expect from my wife?"

Her smile was bitter, her tears hot and frustrated. "Because the ex I told you about was the American equivalent. Andover, Yale, summer home in the Hamptons, racing yacht, a place in investment banking with Daddy. A real Prince Charming. Except he didn't really want a wife. He wanted a decorator. A hostess who could mingle with the best of people and know all those unwritten little rules that keep the social elite separate. He wanted a designer Barbie doll, and no matter how much I loved him, no matter how much I wanted to please him, I wasn't it."

"And you're sure that's what I'd want from you."

Quinn glared at him, frustrated, angry, sad. Wishing with all her heart that Ian could have stayed the nondescript policeman. Wishing she could be the kind of woman who would be happy being whatever he wanted her to be.

"I'm sure that you probably have the most sincere intentions right this minute. And that they'll slowly start to change. I saw it happen with Jason. I saw him build my prison year by year until I barely crawled out with my personality and intelligence intact. I've spent the last few years making sure I don't get stuck in entanglements like that ever again, and I'm not going to give in now."

"Even if you love me."

"Because I love you."

She turned on her heel before he could stop her and stalked down the drive toward the house. She'd thought she'd outrun him. No such luck. When she reached the door, it was his hand that reached out ahead of her and opened it.

"I'm not finished with you yet," he warned.

Quinn came to a shuddering halt, desperate to be away from him. Even more desperate to fold herself back into his arms and let him take care of her. Damn him and his sweet eyes.

"What?" she asked without turning. She felt him behind her, so close she could smell his clean, sharp scent. She could hear his breathing, which was just a little hurried. She almost turned on him, worried suddenly that he'd made his leg worse somehow, that he wasn't feeling well.

She caught herself just in time. That wasn't going to be her job. That was going to be the responsibility of some dim willowy blonde with impeccable taste and a vet's knowledge of the equine world.

"Forget what goes with my name," he suggested. "Tell me why you won't marry *me.*"

"I told you," she said, turning on him. "I have no intentions of becoming a country gentleman's wife and devoting myself to charitable balls and preservation of the species. I don't *want* to be master of the hounds."

Ian's eyebrow quirked. "I don't remember asking you to be."

Quinn plopped a hand on her hip in challenge. "What is your mother?"

"Pardon?"

"What is her most precious achievement in life?"

He paused, his smug expression crumbling a little. "Master of the hounds."

"In that case, I'm sure she'd just adore a daughter-in-law who'd probably teach the future little viscounts to root for the fox."

"I don't think you understand," he objected with commendable calm. "Even my mother has no say over whom I marry."

"But you're a peer, damn it. You have every one of those family portraits breathing down your neck to do the right thing, and it's all up to you. You're the heir to one of the most respected titles in England."

"I had nothing to do with that!" he retorted. "I was perfectly happy being the second son. Safely out of sight, wallowing in the mud with the rest of the second sons. Then Nigel had the bad grace to show off once too often, and everything changed."

"How very inconvenient of him."

"My thought exactly. Because no matter what my parents want or hope, I'll never be the person Nigel was. I'm a copper. I *like* being a copper. My sister's husband, Cecil, is madly happy running the family industries, and I'm more than glad to let him. He does a wonderful job." Ian was yelling at her, his eyes glittering, his voice sharp and taut. The real argument, which they'd been pretending to have the past few days. The real emotion, which was so much more overwhelming than all the imitations. "I have no intentions of being a country gentleman, Quinn. I'm looking for a wife, not a chate-laine.''

"But I don't *want* to be a duchess."

His mouth curved a little. "A countess."

Quinn waved off the correction. "Whatever."

"What do you want to be?"

Two weeks ago she could have answered him. Seven days ago. Now the words froze in her throat, the old goals and new dreams squeezing for room. Ian stood too close to her, crowding her, forcing her in a direction she didn't want to go. She wanted to weaken just for the sake of the yearning in those eyes. She wanted to do anything to keep from hurting him, wanted to be there every time he hurt, every time he stumbled or cried out in the night with the memory of a lost friend. She never wanted Ian to be alone again.

But she couldn't give up all that she was. She couldn't be someone else, even for him. Especially for him, because if she began to travel the same road she had with Jason, she'd end up hating Ian as much as herself for talking her into it. And there could be no worse cruelty.

"I want to be finished with all this business with the hall," was all she could finally say. "Let's go in and talk to Mary."

"Quinn—"

She shook her head, eyes closed, facing the door. "Let's handle her first. Then we can talk. Okay?"

It was a good thing that the hallmark of a good SAS man was being able to retain sound judgment in spite of stress and fatigue, because that was just what Ian was facing. He had a prince to protect, a conference to help coordinate, a ghost to sweet-talk. And all he could think about was how to convince Quinn that she was wrong.

He needed her. Now that he'd been given a taste of what life with her would be like, he couldn't imagine going back to what it was. Fitting as comfortably as he could between two worlds, doing his best to be his own man in a world that judged him by his father's name, his brother's accomplishments. Settling for the future that would be the least objectionable considering the alternatives.

He'd fallen in love with Quinn within the confines of his own expectations, and had badly underestimated her. He'd done her a monumental disservice, and he had to rectify it. Because in exposing him, she'd also shown him what a sham he was. What a smug, pretentious bastard he had been to automatically anticipate that she would emulate the women he'd never respected for being seduced by a title.

She'd wanted him the way he was, the person he sought to be. He had to prove to her that an accident of birth and skiing wouldn't change that. He was the person she'd seen, and not a title or the expectations of every one of his family back to the first baron was going to change it.

"Come on, Mary," Quinn was coaxing, seated on her bed, legs crossed beneath the spread of white skirt, her head upward, Copenhagen on the floor at her feet. "This is serious stuff, hon. We've got a real problem with the hall."

Ian sat in a wing chair over by the window, watching her. This time he was the one with the brandy snifter in his hands.

"Maybe we should wait until dark," he suggested diffidently, since Quinn had been trying already for ten minutes. "Candles and a keening wind, and all that."

"Don't be silly," Quinn objected with a wave of her hand. "Mary never did go in for that sort of stuff. If she's going to pay attention, it'll be here."

"Don't we need a full moon, though?"

"That's only for lovers. Not terrorists."

Ian lifted an eyebrow. "*I'm* not a terrorist."

Quinn glared at him. "Knock it off. We have to get this settled now." Lifting her head, she tried again. "Mary, please. Ian says that these guys could well destroy the hall. They'd sure as hell have guns, and that means any of the villagers could be in danger. Villagers *you* matched up." Silence. "And that doesn't even take into account the animals."

Ian wasn't sure whether it was the way Quinn dragged out that last sentence, implying that Mary would bear the entire brunt of blame if anything happened to her favorite dog, or whether the old biddy was just tired of being paged. Whatever it was, it worked.

Copenhagen lifted his head and began to thump his tail on the floor. The temperature in the room dropped a good fifteen degrees in a matter of seconds. And there, by the door, Ian could have sworn he saw something. Nothing as definite as the night he'd been feverish, nothing he could even describe as white or formed. Just . . . a presence.

Quinn saw it, too. Grinning as if she'd just caught sight of a long-lost friend, she turned to the door. "About time," she chastised the energy. "We can't fool around, now, Mary. We need your help."

Ian heard a sigh, like a wind easing through a cracked window. Except that the windows were closed. Quinn leaned toward the door, her posture intent, her expression serious. Ian tried and failed to think of a way to include this in his official report. He'd be at the giggle academy for certain.

"You see," Quinn was explaining, "Ian is here to organize security for a very important meeting being held here between two warring countries. It's going to be secret because these two countries hate each other so badly they'd try to sabotage the meeting. That means they'd actually try to blow up the hall. Destroy it…" She turned a brief wry smile on Ian. "Trying to couch this in terms relevant to a three-hundred-year-old woman is tough." She turned back to her phantom friend. "Now, I know you have no great love for the royal family. And you do like your practical jokes. But if you do anything during the conference, it could easily set these people off. They could hurt the hall, or the Green. And I don't think you want that to happen."

Ian heard the sighing again, a sad sound, an old sound. He couldn't say why, but he had the feeling that Mary was trying to tell them that she knew only too well what they were trying to say. That she'd seen it all before. She probably had, too. Nobody could play dirty politics like the crowd around the Tudor thrones.

"We need your help, Mary," Quinn went on, perfectly sincere, anxious and earnest, her sympathies obviously with the old woman who had never left her home. "Will you?"

Silence, pulsating in the room like the sound of distant strings. Emptiness. Copenhagen dropped his head again and closed his eyes. The presence was gone, and Ian wondered just what they'd accomplished.

"I wouldn't mind some kind of signature to that promise," Quinn said, still facing the doorway.

Nothing.

She sighed and turned Ian's way. "What do you think?"

He shrugged and drained the rest of his brandy. "I think it's the best we're going to do."

"Are you sure it's enough?"

He got to his feet. "I'm afraid it's going to have to be. I happen to work for a rather pragmatic lot that doesn't put much stock in ghosts. They're still wagering on electronics and weaponry and quick transportation."

"Are you going to be here?" Quinn asked, her feet dangling over the side of the high bed. She looked very much like a schoolgirl on holiday.

"At least while the prince is, certainly. The rest is up to the other chaps."

She dipped her head a little, her forehead drawn, her hands flat on the bed on either side of her. "And you promise to take care of yourself?"

"I'll have to, won't I?" he asked with a wry smile. "My nurse isn't going to be here to take care of me if I don't."

She looked up at him, her eyes dark with the memory of those hours. The fear, the care, the terrible uncertainty. He loved her all the more for her courage to face something that daunting and not flinch from it. He ached with the fierce anguish of a man who saw something he'd never imagined he could have slip out of his grasp.

"Come along," he coaxed, a hand out to her. "The two of us are going to be on our ears if we don't get some nourishment. I'll treat you to any pub lunch in town."

She shied from him, folded into herself just a little, as if summoning courage, or protection. Finally, her eyes naked and vulnerable in their ambivalence, she stepped onto the low stool at the side of the bed, and held out her hand to him. She was halfway up, most of her weight on the stool, when one of its legs gave out.

Quinn gave a little cry and flailed for balance. Halfway across the room, Ian dropped his glass and reached for her. The snifter shattered into fragments on the wood floor. Quinn toppled from the stool. Ian caught her just before she fell.

Her eyes were wide. Her lips were parted. That telltale color at the base of her throat gave her away. Ian should have let her go. He should have put her back on her feet and guided her on out the door. Instead, he gathered her fully into his arms and kissed her.

She struggled for an instant, more surprised than outraged. Her hands came up to his shoulders, flat against him as if she were going to push. She never did. Within the space of a heartbeat, she melted against him. Her lips, parted in alarm, widened in invitation. She moaned, a soft entreaty that shattered the rest of Ian's reserves. When her arms slipped around his neck, Ian lifted her back onto the bed.

Somewhere behind him, on a wind through a window that wasn't open, came the sound of a soft chuckle.

Thirteen

"**T**his doesn't change things," Quinn insisted, even though she couldn't stop smiling.

Her toes were tingling. Her fingers were tingling. Her belly glowed with the sweet aftermath of lovemaking. Thorough lovemaking. Gentle lovemaking. The kind of lovemaking that friends, fond lovers, share.

Ian's head rested against her chest. She could feel the even brush of his breath on her breasts, the soft caress of his hair on her skin. She could still taste brandy, and thought she liked it better in a kiss than in a balloon glass.

That made her smile again.

"You're not listening," she insisted, nudging Ian.

He didn't even open his eyes. "It changes everything," he argued lazily. "I've compromised you. Therefore I'm obliged to do the honorable thing and marry you."

Quinn giggled, bouncing Ian around a bit. "This isn't a Regency novel, old boy. If it were, I'd just be a weak-willed trollop with a taste for blond viscounts."

"Ah, but you are," he countered easily and earned himself a good cuffing in the ear. "I know your type," he accused just as affably. "Make up to a guy while he seems to be a regular working stiff just on the off chance he's got a title and an in-heritance he's forgotten to tell you about.''

"That's me," she sighed. "Blinded by the chance to have my very own tiara."

"You would, you know."

Quinn shut her eyes and knew that Ian could feel the sud-den staccato of her heart. Fear, distress, anxiety. "I don't suppose you could just turn it all down," she tried, eyes still closed, her hands cupping Ian to her.

"Not bloody likely," he said, "with Gervase the Sot wait-ing patiently in the wings. My family is much less forgiving than the Windsors about that sort of thing."

"That's what I was afraid of."

Ian lifted his head, then faced her with an expression that was far more serious than his words. His forehead was creased, that wonderfully wry cant to his eyebrows absent.

"Can I tell you a story?" he asked.

Quinn's heart raced even faster. "Go ahead."

He nodded and pulled himself up so that he was resting against the pillows alongside her. "There was once a little boy," he said, "raised in a very nice, rather large house by a nanny. His parents were very proper parents of the type. Trained him in the nursery, sent him away to school at six, saw him at the odd holiday and encouraged him to do the proper thing with his life. Since he was only the second son, he wouldn't inherit, but he would be obliged to live up to the family's expectations. His choices for gainful employment were the collar or the saber. Wisely, because of his basic tem-perament, he chose the saber. Distressed his family when he opted to read at Oxford instead of slog through Sandhurst. Outraged them completely when he chucked the family regi-ment for a branch of the service that eschewed stuffy things like titles or privilege of rank. They most certainly didn't ap-prove when the second son found that he liked being a mav-erick among other mavericks, but at least he was in an honorable profession."

"But then the Falklands."

"Um, as a matter of fact, no."

Quinn turned on him to see the rueful smile she'd come to know so well. She scowled at him. "Now what?" she de-manded.

"Well, that lad *was* in the Falklands. Did find himself in close company with a certain prince at times."

"Did he, in fact, earn the Military Cross?"

His scowl was purely British, totally self-effacing. "I suppose he did, yes. But he didn't do all that damage to his leg there. That happened in a little known place called Q'rat. Antiterrorist raid."

Quinn almost stopped breathing. "Good God. You mean that your friend Brian died in Q'rat?"

His eyes darkened with the pain, still so fresh that it escaped in dreams and nightmares. Quinn wanted to soothe it for him. She wanted to take it from him.

"And they're asking you to attend this conference?"

Ian shrugged. "It's my job," he said. "I, um, know the territory."

"But that's cruel!"

He smiled at her, lifted a hand to cup her cheek. "I'll have to have you discuss my future assignments for me. The point of the story is that, after that, the lad decided that he still rather liked being a maverick. So, instead of going into business in the city with his brother-in-law, or back to the regular regiment where his uncle, the previous second son, still served, he fought his way onto the police force."

"With a limp."

He shrugged. "It doesn't usually slow me down. Especially in the Yard, because what I do is mostly investigate. Anyway, when the lad's older brother decided to test his mortality once too often, the young inspector suddenly found himself a viscount with a nervous mother, distressed father and a ready-to-wear future, if he wanted it. The brother's title, his inheritance, his aspirations, even his fiancée if he chose."

"Convenient."

He nodded, pulled her against him. "The lad knew he had to accept most of the package. That's just the way things were. But the fiancée was a different story. She was just the person his parents would want, the person his brother would have wanted—did want. But the young lad, now an inspector, found that he'd grown restless with the prospect of his new life. He wanted more, and he wasn't sure what it was. All he was sure of was that it wasn't the veritable sea of respectable young ladies his mother had been parading past him since the moment the black-bordered announcement appeared in the *Times,* or the quiet upstanding sort of life those ladies proposed.''

"Enter the weak-willed trollop."

"Exactly. I never knew exactly how I was going to balance my needs and the demands of the title. How I'd know when I was in danger of surrendering. You're absolutely right. It's a matter of degrees. A slow slide into oblivion begun out of love and obligation. But I can't do that. I can't offer myself up just because I'm expected to. If I'd wanted to do that, I would have been a cleric. And within minutes of meeting you, I knew that you were my answer." His eyes softened, darkened, smiled. "You can save me, Quinn."

She wanted to turn away, to protect herself from the appeal in those eyes. She wanted so badly to believe him, believe that he would be strong enough to withstand the pressures being placed on him. She wanted to think that in fifteen years, in forty years, Ian would still think of himself as an inspector, instead of an earl.

"I don't know," she hedged, even though she did.

She had to talk to Allison. She had to talk to Morwena, steeping herself in the wisdom of women—married women— who had once been where she was. Who had to make a decision for their lives, for the lives of the men they loved and the children they would produce together. She had to know whether she'd be strong enough to withstand an even greater wind than the one Ian battled, because they would never accept her, not really.

Not that she particularly cared. But Ian would. And if she was going to make the kind of commitment that would eventually mean children, she would never allow those children to be separated from the people who were their heritage.

"Think about it," Ian coaxed, pulling her against him, his hand in her hair, his cheek against her forehead. "I can give you so much."

Quinn stiffened instinctively. "What can you give me?"

She could feel his smile. "A future," he said. "A past. An old house with the echoes of children's laughter in it, where you can still smell the lavender of pomanders and the spice of a Yule log. Where traditions are centuries old. Where we'd have children of our own to carry on our names."

She knew he could feel her tears trickle down his neck. He couldn't have given her a more perfect answer. All she'd ever wanted. All she could ever hope for.

"I can't quit my work," she told him, wrapping her arm tightly around his chest, needing that purchase, that stability, needing his strength if she was to have any of her own.

"I wouldn't want you to. Of course, unless the palace asks you personally, I think you might consider working exclusively for Heritage House."

"Are you sure?" she asked with a grin. "Don't you think the board might consider it a conflict of interest?"

"I doubt it. I'm chairman of the board."

She held on tighter, soaking in the soothing hush of his breathing, the steady throb of his heart. Possibility, probability. The question of a future balanced against the misfortunes of the past.

"Ian?"

"Yes, love."

"I'm scared."

He stroked her hair, his fingers gentle and nurturing. "If it'll help, I'm willing to make one huge concession."

"What's that?"

"I won't say more till after the conference. We can go home to Malham then. Test the waters, see how we both fare."

Home. Such a promise to a wanderer like her. So evocative. Malham would be hers, to treasure, to protect, to preserve. More importantly, she would have a sense of permanence. Someone to greet at the end of the day, someone to wake up to. Ian. The most exhilarating, frightening, comforting thought of all. Quinn took a deep breath and broke every promise she'd made to herself in the last few years.

"It's a deal," she said.

They had two days of peace. No surprises, no invasions, no new problems. Quinn scheduled her priorities and made finishing touches. Ian consulted with London and began filling in diagrams and equipment requests. He kept his promise about not pressuring her, and they enjoyed their free time walking the beach or visiting the village for an evening of darts and racing on the telly.

While walking, Ian finally told her the story of how his friend Brian Willingsgate had died. How they had been called to free hostages held at a distant airport, only to find themselves in the middle of a full-scale attack.

The SAS worked in four-man teams, with the men partnering, much like police. Brian had been Ian's partner. The big, bluff redheaded farmer's son had refused to leave Ian when an exploding grenade had shattered Ian's hip. He had protected him as long as possible, surrendering to the terrorists only to save Ian's life.

Slowly, his voice faltering over words he'd never shared with anyone, Ian related the hours he'd fought to free himself, how he'd watched Brian systematically tortured. How he'd killed a woman bare-handed trying to save Brian's life. How, even though he'd done everything he could, dragging Brian out himself, stealing a truck and escaping to an international compound, it had been too late.

Ian's telling was blunt and factual, his own actions downplayed. Even so, strolling along the beach with only the gulls and the wash of the wind for company, Quinn heard the echoes of fury, terror, the relentless screaming of fanatics. She could smell the blood, hear the desperation of a man who wanted only to protect his friend. She couldn't even imagine the strength of will that had carried Ian back out of that crowded, airless little room, his friend's unconscious body over his shoulder, his leg useless.

She couldn't believe that his was a family that wouldn't prize above all the courage and loyalty of their son. That they could ever find this self-effacing hero wanting.

She thought maybe that, because they might, they would never really understand Ian. And that maybe it would take someone who did understand him to protect him from them. Someone who didn't see herself in terms of social order or family affiliations.

It amused her to think that she was actually looking forward to the weekend at Malham. After all, once a person's done battle with a dead countess, what kind of challenge could a live one be?

The second evening, Ian and the colonel gathered several of the town elders down at the Three Horseshoes to begin filling them in about the summit. Quinn stayed back at the hall, seeing to a shipment of china that had been delivered that day. She loved unwrapping each delicate piece of Spode and cleaning it herself. It was sort of a ritual of completion for her, the final few preparations before the house was to be opened.

Tomorrow Ian was making her move into town with Morwena. They hadn't received any new specific threats, but the security people would be arriving the next day, which signaled the real beginning of things. Quinn just hoped that that great pack of oafs didn't break something delicate in the house.

She was elbow deep in suds and humming when the front bell chimed. Pulling the towel from her shoulder, she deserted the half-filled sink and began the long march to the front of the house. A check of the clock showed that it was still early. She'd figured that planning session to last at least until last call. And then the two old military planners had to find their way back home. But of course, they had Copenhagen.

Quinn was grinning with a certain amount of tolerance when she unlatched the door and pulled it open.

"Oh. Good evening."

It wasn't Ian and the colonel after all. A black Daimler sat beside the pond, and five visitors crowded the steps. All wore their best spring attire—brown tweed coats, perky little hats, and brollies, ruthlessly rolled into lethal-looking silhouettes.

"Mrs. Bumphries," Quinn greeted the lady in the lead. "Won't you come in?"

"Thank you, my dear," the rigid little woman answered with a nod of her head and a quick adjustment to the purse hanging from her forearm. Great purse, Quinn thought inconsequentially as the little band trooped up the steps and into the foyer. You could pack the thing for a tour of the Orient.

Three men and another woman followed Mrs. Bumphries, all well past mid-life crisis, all severe and earnest, all buttoned up and proper, their sensible shoes squeaking a bit on the marble flooring.

"What can I do for you this evening?" Quinn asked as she moved to close the door against the chilly night air. Mrs. Bumphries must have gotten a new chauffeur. Quinn had met the previous driver, the tall rawboned Billy. The man who leaned against the Daimler was shorter, darker. Pulling out a cigarette, he smiled in answer to Quinn's vague greeting as she swung the door shut.

"Is he here, then?" Mrs. Bumphries asked in that perfectly precise voice of hers, crossing her gloved hands across her stomach like a teacher waiting to begin a lesson.

Quinn turned to them, wondering what they needed the colonel for. Probably another assault on landowners everywhere to protect helpless Norwegian rats from exterminators or something.

"The colonel?" she asked with a smile. "No, I'm afraid you've missed him. He's down at the Horseshoes with Mr. Matthews right now."

"Not the colonel," the little woman retorted with severely pursed features. "His Royal Highness. The prince."

Quinn looked from one earnest face to another. "Who?"

"Knew they'd come through, of course," the colonel was saying as he strode along beside Ian. "Splendid chaps."

All the walking lately must have been doing him some good, Ian decided. His leg felt stronger than it had for months, which put him in a good mood. The meeting had gone well, the village officials taking the news about the upcoming summit with admirable calm. The plans were complete, the team arriving in the morning and Quinn off to the village where she'd be safe.

Tonight the moors rustled with the wind and the small animals who lived in the hedgerows. The sky was fading to mauve, and soon the moon would rise. Off to the left, the sea murmured endlessly. Ian allowed a real feeling of satisfaction to pervade him. A sense of anticipation. The end of the assignment was in sight, and after that he could tackle his future.

"Looks like somebody's at the hall," the colonel observed.

Ian immediately snapped to attention. They were topping the rise, the trees shushing around them, the cowbells clanking in the distance. A few lights were on in the house, and on the other side of the pond sat a black Daimler. Ian instinctively reached around for his gun. It was there, tucked beneath his jacket, just as it had been since the last round of threats.

"Quinn wasn't expecting anyone," Ian countered, his voice already soft, his brain in gear, his stomach abruptly on fire.

"Oh, damn it all," Alistair suddenly blurted, taking Ian's attention. "I know who it is. Letitia Bumphries. She's been after me to make one of her Gentle Friends of Small Creatures meetings, and I've been doing my best to avoid her. Blasted nuisance, that woman."

Ian's hand dropped. Something nudged his brain, but he couldn't pull it free.

"Door to her car's open."

Alistair shook his head. "She must have forgotten to close it. Usually her chauffeur drives her. She's frightfully forgetful otherwise."

Alistair leaned into the car to check it, then closed the door. The dome light flicked off, leaving the lawn dark except for the shafts of light spilling from the study on one side and the drawing room on the other. The two men were about to walk up the steps. For some reason, Copenhagen, who had been trotting alongside in companionable silence, suddenly went down on his belly and began to growl.

Alistair stopped. "I say, old man. What's wrong?"

Ian's hand went once again to his gun. Copenhagen never took his attention off the door, still growling low in his throat. Ian held up a hand to silently caution the colonel and edged around to a window, his hackles up. He could hear a low moaning, as if someone were injured. The sound seemed to come from inside the house.

Ian stepped up to the window, his gun drawn, and peered inside.

"Bloody hell."

He could see six people, arranged in an odd tableau. One of them, the thin old lady with the huge purse, was talking and looking over her shoulder. The rest watched her. Quinn sat on the Chippendale chair, and her arms were tied behind her back.

"Who did you say that woman was?" Ian demanded, crouching back by the colonel.

"Letitia Bumphries. Of the Gentle Friends of Small Creatures—"

"Small creatures," Ian echoed, searching for the significance. When it came, it was almost embarrassing. "That's it!" he snapped, rubbing his face to keep from laughing. "That's bloody well it. God, I can't believe it. *Those* are our terrorists."

"What are you talking about, man?"

Taking a slow breath to give himself time to think, Ian took a quick assessing look around and turned back to Alistair. "Colonel, what do you say to going out for a little nip of something?"

Ferrets. She was going to die for ferrets. Quinn couldn't believe it. Of all the ridiculous reasons to be tied up and threatened, it had to be the fact that some king in a country five thousand miles away kept a couple of pet rodents in a gold cage.

Mrs. Bumphries had been unfailingly polite. She really didn't want to hurt Quinn. She had great respect and appreciation for the work Quinn was doing, restoring a treasure like Hartley Hall. But unfortunately, she knew the prince was coming, and she needed to get a message to him. A message certainly the prince would understand and agree with—that no animal should be kept in a cage, no matter how pretty, simply because a person wanted to look at it all day.

There were people out there who gave no thought to abusing a helpless animal simply for a person's own pleasure, and it was the Gentle Friends' duty to notify the world of it. And since no one had really paid enough attention to them so far, even with the roadblocks and Quilting for Bees they'd arranged, they had decided, upon finding out to their good fortune that a royal visit was due, that they simply could not waste the opportunity.

Quinn had patiently listened to the diminutive Mrs. Bumphries talk about what she needed to tell the prince, all the time wondering how the woman had known the prince was even coming, and then Quinn had tried her best to get the little gathering back out the door. That had been when Mrs. Bumphries had pulled the Uzi on her.

The other four commandos followed her lead, producing their guns from briefcases, coats and knitting bags. The rope had been in that steamer trunk over Mrs. Bumphries's arm, along with a pile of pamphlets, a steel trap, several small red sweaters, a copy of *Royal* magazine and seven clips of ammunition. Quinn was being held hostage by a band of cutthroats who wielded automatic weapons and umbrellas.

"No one takes us seriously," their leader was saying, gesturing first with her brolly and then with her gun. Quinn sincerely hoped that neither accidently went off. "They think we're just harmless eccentrics. Well, they'll think differently now."

"How did you find out, Mrs. Bumphries?" Quinn asked, carefully pulling again at her bonds. Mr. Wilby had tied her up, but his arthritis prevented him from doing a very strong knot. He'd said that they were counting on the Uzis to keep Quinn still, anyway. Quinn was counting on the knots falling apart sometime soon.

"Why, Colonel Smythe-Smithe, dear," Mrs. Bumphries replied. "He's so very pleased that His Royal Highness is actually coming here, he had to tell somebody."

Quinn's smile was pained. "So he told you."

She smiled. "Of course, dear. Whyever not?"

Because you're nuts? Quinn thought. Because you might be dotty enough to try to take an empty country house hostage because you hadn't quite got the dates right? The five of them had recited "Thirty days hath September..." for fifteen minutes trying to figure out how they'd miscalculated the length of the last month and missed the prince. Then they'd decided that they'd just wait for him to show up.

Miss Prim had been dispatched to check the larder and come back with the depressing news that there was meat being stored there. Another sin in the eyes of the Gentle Friends, evidently. They would, Mrs. Bumphries announced grandly, survive on biscuits and tea.

"Are you going to hold the prince hostage?" Quinn asked. She wasn't doing anything else. She might as well at least get details. Just in case the colonel and Ian found their way back home from the pub and stumbled in on this mess.

"Oh, no, my dear, of course not. Only you. And the colonel and Mr. Matthews. We would never actually *threaten* a member of the royal family. Why, that would be treason."

"What about the peerage?" she asked, willing to try anything.

Mrs. Bumphries did a quick check of her fellow terrorists and came away with vague shakes of heads. "Why, I don't know," she admitted. "We've never really discussed it, have we?"

Four answering shakes of heads.

Quinn gave it the old college try. "Well, if you do this, you will be taking a peer hostage. We found out the other day that Mr. Matthews is actually the Viscount Giggleswick, you know. His father's Lord Malham. I mean, you couldn't just go around shooting a presumptive earl."

Mrs. Bumphries just smiled. "I think I'd know a viscount when I see one, Miss Rutledge. Mr. Matthews doesn't have nearly the panache of the real Viscount Giggleswick."

"Oh, no," Quinn retorted. "That one's dead. Ian is the *other* Viscount Giggleswick."

"She's right, Letitia," Mr. Wilby said. "At least about the viscount. He died skiing. Don't you remember? We jotted it down in our Debrett's."

Oh, God, Quinn thought. Preserve me from armed eccentrics. Come on, Mary. Do something. Quinn thought she'd heard a warm-up moan a minute ago, but it had been quiet since. One good blast from Mary would send this crowd screaming for the hills. Unfortunately the old countess seemed to be tuned out. Probably taking Quinn and Ian at their word and not stirring up any trouble. Quinn hoped that Ian would somehow know something was wrong, that he could save the day before one of these old dears accidently shot her.

She'd no sooner thought it than she heard it. The heavy slam of the door, uneven footsteps and the first twelve bars of "Lydia the Tattooed Lady." Badly out of tune and delivered with uncustomary gusto.

"Oh, well, so much for the cavalry."

There was nothing to do but hang her head in shame.

Fourteen

———

"Well, what have we here?" Ian bellowed, stumbling over the hall table and chuckling. "Visitors?"

Even from where she sat, Quinn could smell the whiskey.

"Mr. Matthews," Mrs. Bumphries greeted him, the Uzi held out in front of her like a sword. The brolly in her other hand looked much deadlier. He didn't seem to notice either. "I'm pleased to see that you're feeling better."

"Better?" he echoed and teetered into the room. "I'm *won*derful! Bloody paralyzed. And who the hell are you?"

He was reeling in the doorway, his hands out to the sides as if searching for balance, his jacket hanging off one shoulder and his hair sticking out at odd angles. His eyes were wavering as badly as he was, and his voice dipped and soared in an awesome display of versatility.

"I am Letitia Bumphries, of the Gentle Friends of Small Creatures of Albion," she introduced herself quite properly. "I'm the spokeswoman for our little group."

"Good," he allowed with a slow nod of his head as he edged his way into the room where the five people stood in an untidy cluster to Quinn's right. "Smashing." He struggled to focus on her. "The spokeswoman, you say."

By now he was very close to the band. They were watching him much the way they might an Elvis impersonator.

"Yes," Letitia answered, straightening a little, shifting the Uzi as if she'd been moving to fold her hands again.

He nodded, seemingly oblivious to Quinn's glare. "Excellent. Brilliant. In that case, I imagine you can answer me a question."

"If you pose it properly."

He came to a stop not two feet away from her, smiling giddily. Several of the Gentle Friends smiled back.

"Do you," he asked, "have any idea how a safety mechanism works on an Uzi?"

Surprised, she looked down at the gun in her hand. "Why, no. We don't."

He nodded, suddenly brisk. "Good. Because yours are all on."

And as they looked down to check, he neatly swept each gun out of uncertain hands and headed for Quinn.

"Are you all right?" he asked, allowing his first true emotion of the encounter. He was, of course, dead sober.

Quinn giggled and spread her arms wide. The ropes promptly fell onto the floor. "I was more afraid of an accident than anything."

"Oh, dear," Mrs. Bumphries mourned, her hands finally comfortably folded over each other, the umbrella hung next to the purse. "Does this mean the prince won't speak to us?"

At that moment, the colonel leapt through the door, his Purdy shotgun poised for action. Ian and Quinn ducked. The rest turned slightly and smiled as if he'd just entered for tea. The tableau held, the shotgun unwavering in the colonel's hands, the terrorists waiting like a choir for their bus. Then the colonel caught sight of the store of weaponry in Ian's hands and relaxed with an indignant huff.

"Could have left something for me to do, what?"

"I fully expected resistance, Colonel," Ian assured him. "That's why I asked you to attempt the flanking maneuver."

"Crawled up that damn priest hole," he groused, breaking down the gun. "Just in case they'd gained purchase in the great hall." Coming to complete parade attention, he glared down his nose at the little woman at the head of the pack.

"Letitia, I'm ashamed of you. What do you mean, threatening a prince?"

"We wouldn't do that," the woman explained again. "Merely you. We knew you wouldn't mind so very much. And Mr. Matthews. Did you know, Alistair, that Miss Rutledge has been insisting that Mr. Matthews is actually the Viscount Giggleswick? Isn't that the boldest thing?"

The gun resting over his forearm as if he were just heading out after a grouse, the colonel gave a loud harrumph. "He *is* the viscount, woman. And you very nearly endangered his life."

And much to Quinn's eternal amazement, that was what provoked the most real emotion in the group. Mouths gaped. Skin paled. Several small gasps of dismay were heard, and Letitia sank down into one of the chairs.

"Oh, I'm ever so sorry, my lord," she apologized breathlessly. "I had no idea—"

"Who gave you the guns, Mrs. Bumphries?" Ian asked as he carefully slid the clips from every gun but one.

She looked up at him with vague eyes. "Why, Ahmed, of course. He was ever so clever about the whole thing."

Ian stiffened. "Ahmed?"

"My chauffeur. He's been with me since Billy took off for parts unknown. Don't know what I'd do without him, don't you know."

"Where is he now?" Ian asked.

"Why, outside, of course. He carried the weapons in the boot of the auto until we arrived. He said he'd wait for us.... Oh, dear. I suppose I should let him know."

Ian was already dropping three of the Uzis into Quinn's hand. "I think he knows already," he assured the old lady, turning to leave. "Colonel, let's go."

Mary wasn't absent, after all. Ian had no sooner holstered his own gun and pocketed extra clips for the Uzi than the front door slammed open. Everyone jumped. Quinn heard an engine, then the crunch of gravel.

Ahmed was taking off. Ahmed who had supplied the guns. Ian was out the study door before anyone else could move. Quinn ran after him. The colonel followed, twisting the Purdy back into position.

It turned out that Mary hadn't been at all lax. Quinn reached the front door to find Blackie waiting down at the bottom of the steps.

"How'd he get there?" she demanded.

"I don't know," Ian answered, swinging up on the horse's back. "But I don't look a gift horse in the mouth. Call the police. Have them get a bomb squad out to search. I'm going after our chauffeur."

"But Ian," she protested, "he's driving. And it's getting dark."

Ian's smile was piratical. One hand in Blackie's mane, the other holding the gun, he looked like a highwayman. Right on cue, Blackie reared on his back legs, his whinny rocketing off the stone wall.

"The man's undoubtedly crippled the other cars," Ian yelled down at her, easily riding out the tantrum. "Besides, I can make it across the field in half the time he can by road. I've got the best chaser on the island."

"And a leg that's held on with bailing wire. Ian, don't!"

She should have known better. With a shout, Ian brought Blackie around and turned him down the drive. Hoofbeats clattered across the gravel. Quinn stood at the door, mesmerized by the sight, Ian crouched over the neck of that horse as if he were more an extension of the animal than a rider, the power and grace of their flight breathtaking. Briefly she thought of what Ian must have been like when he raced. And she knew that he would never be the earl his father thought he should be.

Then she turned back into the house to make the calls. At the last minute, something Ian had said galvanized her. Spinning toward his retreating form, she gasped, "A bomb?"

A bomb. Probably Ahmed's real reason for inciting the ladies to try their abortive raid, the Scotland Yard gentleman said to her over the phone when she explained. A camouflaging maneuver so he could plant something to really damage the conference while everyone was slapping the hands of well-intentioned but misguided little old ladies.

Prompt action was promised and received. Helicopters swept over the fields within fifteen minutes of her call, and sirens keened and whooped almost before she had her hand off the phone.

Quinn didn't wait long enough to greet the first wave. She let the greatly chastened Gentle Friends do that. The minute she heard the crisp affirmative from the police, she and the colonel took off in their own pursuit.

Ahmed had, in fact, disabled Quinn's Mini and Ian's Lotus, but fortunately Quinn knew even more about cars than she did old houses. She and the colonel split the remaining ammunition and squeeled out of the estate in the Lotus with a gravel-spitting turn just as the flashing blue lights appeared over the hill from the other direction.

A man on a horse against a Daimler, Quinn kept thinking, downshifting and honking as she swept around one blind corner after another. The odds just weren't good enough on that one, especially if the man in the Daimler was armed. She had no doubt he was.

"I hope they didn't turn off," she said aloud, honking again, double clutching and praying that she had imagined the brief glimpse of oncoming headlights. There just wasn't that much room on these roads to hit these corners at this speed and hope to get by a Range Rover. Over in the passenger seat, the colonel alternately clutched the door, his Purdy and his chest.

"I hope I'm alive when we reach them," he said fervently.

Quinn couldn't resist a small grin. "I'm depending on you to help Ian," she told him. "I have no idea how to fire one of these."

The colonel shot her an arch look. "Then why didn't you stay back at the hall and wait for the police the way I told you to, young lady?"

She just shook her head. "I hate waiting."

Suddenly everything changed. There, stabbing the deepening dusk, were a pair of headlights. Quinn downshifted the car until it whined in protest. Then she heard the whinnying and knew she'd found them. Her heart slammed into her ribs.

"Showtime," she muttered.

She needn't have worried. Rounding the last corner, she brought the Lotus to a halt just beyond the gate to Morgan Farnworth's place and cut the engine. Beside her the colonel straightened, fondled his gun and let out a bark of amusement.

"Well done," he snapped in approval and opened his door.

Their lights mingled with the Daimler's to illuminate Blackie and Ahmed dead center in the road, their positions more than familiar to anyone who'd had been at the hall during Blackie's reign. The little man was sobbing, the horse whinnying, his hooves striking sparks within inches of the chauffeur's rolled-up body. At the side of the road Ian lounged against the hood of the Daimler where it had come to rest at an odd angle against a hedgerow. The gun was in his hand, his arms crossed over his chest, his legs crossed at the ankles.

"Are you going to help him?" Quinn asked as she stepped from the driver's side, her casual tone belying the thunder of her heart.

He was safe. He was upright. But even with his passive expression, Quinn could see that the ride had cost him. The line of his jaw was as tight as wire. He was pale, and sweat glistened on his forehead. But, she knew, it could wait. He had succeeded.

Ian's first reaction to seeing her was outrage. A risk taker's instinctive protectiveness of civilians. Her purposeful calm took a lot of the starch right back out of his stance, though. Lifting a wry eyebrow at her, he turned back to where he'd been considering the shrieking Ahmed as he rolled across the road, arms over his head, the horse snorting and stamping above him.

"Oh, only if he hurts a hoof or something."

Quinn hardly recognized him in the dying light of day. Same Ian, same casual elegance, same instinctive assurance. But there was a fire in him tonight, a scorching life that Quinn had never seen before. His eyes shone. He couldn't stop smiling. Even leaning nonchalantly, arms folded, hurting enough that he couldn't put any weight on his bad leg, he looked as restless as his horse.

Alive. Really alive. The essence of Ian Matthews George Elliott Spears-Wykeham, the Viscount Giggleswick.

"I say, Giggleswick," the colonel bellowed, shotgun still balanced on his arm as if they were on the way out for grouse. "Well done. *Well* done."

"Do you mean to tell me you left the terrorists behind?" Ian demanded without much heat. "After all we went through to apprehend them?"

Quinn walked up to him, careful to stay out of Blackie's way. "They're preparing tea and biscuits for the police. Has Ahmed said anything about the bomb?"

It was interesting that for all the noise and movement, Blackie hadn't touched the cowering man. Quinn turned to watch the action as she leaned her own rump against the car. Ian didn't do more than change the gun to his other hand when Quinn slid an arm around his waist.

"As a matter of fact," he said, wrapping his own deceptively casual-looking arm around her shoulder, "he tells me that it's in the Dungeon Snug. Radio-activated to be detonated sometime during the summit. He was hoping that the activities of the Gentle Friends would effectively masquerade his real purpose."

The colonel had joined them by now, the shotgun still poised over his arm. "Are you going to let Blackie finish him off?" he asked. "Or just play with him a bit?"

"No," Ian replied. "I suppose he's had quite enough. If you'd be so good, Colonel..."

Ian motioned to the gun, and the colonel responded with alacrity, shouldering it and coming to attention. Turning his attention back to the scene across the road, Ian let out a quick shrill whistle. Immediately Blackie came back down on all fours and stood stock-still. Ahmed, obviously waiting for a repeat performance, chose to remain where he was.

"How did you stop him?" Quinn asked, readjusting her position just enough to take more of Ian's weight.

"I whistled."

"Not the horse. Ahmed."

Ian shrugged. "Rode up alongside him. Did a bit of close-up persuasion through the window."

"Wizard," the colonel breathed in awe.

"Stupid," Quinn countered dryly.

All three of them looked up at the approaching thump-thump of helicopters.

"Should we go back?" Alistair asked.

"No," Ian decided. "No need to go charging about when they'll all be here soon enough, anyway."

Quinn just shook her head. Considering how much of Ian's weight she was now supporting, how very strained his face was beneath that nonchalant voice, she couldn't believe how composed he was. The colonel would probably never understand that Ian wasn't going back because he couldn't get there.

"What?" a new voice demanded. "Didn't save any of the fun for us, you poncy sod?"

Quinn turned to see a group of shadows detach themselves from a nearby hedgerow. She imagined they were in camouflage, but in the deepening dusk they looked as if they'd stood under the same chimney flue Ian had. Every one of them held up a small, flat black weapon that looked similar to the one in Ian's hands, and their cartridge belts held any number of extra toys. Crepe-soled soles swallowed the sounds of their footsteps along the macadam.

Ian immediately straightened to greet them. "Barnes?" he demanded, obviously delighted. "What's wrong? All the real soldiers busy? I suppose that's that paid-off cripple, Webster, with you."

"And lucky you are it is, too, mate," one of the others answered with a face-splitting grin. "Fancy that, callin' me outa my nice warm supper to save some bum-faced viscount. Giggleswick, they say. Giggleswick? says I. I ain't savin' nobody named Giggleswick. He's probably one of them bleedin' sheepherders from Yorkshire."

"This," Quinn asked with a wry grin, "is the famous SAS?"

All four men turned to her with affronted expressions.

"Hasn't been the same since I left," Ian said with a grin of his own.

"Cheeky bird," Webster allowed.

"Watch your tongue, boyo," Ian warned affably. "That cheeky bird is going to be the next Viscountess Giggleswick."

Quinn winced. "Giggleswick," she mourned with a shake of her head. "It has to be Giggleswick, huh?"

The laughter was thunderous, the back-slapping torturous and Quinn's reputation among Ian's friends forever set. By the time they loaded Ahmed into a helicopter and Ian into their jeep for the ride back to the hall, Quinn was already considered one of the family. By the time she tucked Blackie into his box and Ian into his bed, she'd already made up her mind about the outcome of her visit to Malham Hall. She might have said something to Ian, but the codeine he finally agreed to take made conversation a bit one-sided. She decided to wait. After all, they still had to get through the conference.

Malham Hall. The quintessential English country manor, first seeing life as a convent and then country showplace for a series of political favorites, ending up with the Spears-Wykehams after they'd backed Henry Tudor at Bosworth.

Successive generations had consolidated power and expanded the original plan until the fourth earl had seen the work being done at Castle Howard and employed the talents of John Vanbrugh. Since then, only minor renovations had changed the actual shape and style of the house, so that instead of looking like a badly compiled collection of architectural whims, it gleamed with a classic purity.

Quinn admitted to spending the first forty-eight hours within its park boarders in a constant state of awe. Her neck ached from examining the murals that crowded the dining room and Queen Anne drawing room. She almost completely missed luncheon because she was seated on the floor of the great gallery in the west wing thinking that this was really what a great gallery should be.

The house was more than she could have dreamed; Ian's family was less.

It wasn't that she was particularly uncomfortable with them. She'd renovated her way through too many aristocratic homes not to know how to act. It was just that no matter how much she might have wanted otherwise, she was probably the last person on earth they wanted Ian to marry. They were exceedingly polite and passionately correct. They were also very upset.

Ian was everything she could have wished. Attentive, considerate, comfortable. When he'd finally discovered her seated cross-legged in the middle of the eighty-foot length of paintings and statues and green silk wallpaper when she should have been scooping at her melon, he promptly sat down beside her and followed her gaze.

"Like it?" he asked, grinning.

She didn't even look over at him. "Don't be a pig. That Vermeer up there belongs to *you.*"

He shrugged. "To the trust."

She shook her head. "My first instinct is that if it were mine I wouldn't want to share it with anyone. My second instinct is that it's a crime hiding it away here."

"And the Van Dyke?"

"And the Stubbs, and the Turner and the Reynolds."

"I know," he admitted, following her gaze. "I agree."

She turned to him. "You're going to open the house?"

He shrugged. "It might never be my decision to make. But this is as much a part of England as Warwick Castle and Blenheim Palace."

She took hold of his hand. "Your family doesn't agree."

"Even the Queen has people going through her house when she's not home."

Quinn shook her head a little, amazed. "Well, after all. You're going to be in London, with Scotland Yard, most of the time, anyway."

"As a matter of fact," he answered with a smile, "I am."

Not according to his mother. According to the Countess of Malham, it was Ian's duty to follow in his father's footsteps. There were family responsibilities to consider for now, companies and estates and traditions to learn. Then, of course, House of Lords. Member of the board on any number of worthy causes. Ian liked racing—let him be on the board of the Jockey Club, or the Hunt Committee. He was, after all, not just anybody.

Even the palace's personal thanks for a job well-done on a successful summit hadn't changed matters. Spears-Wykehams were simply not policemen, not even policemen to the crown.

Lady Malham was one of those relentlessly efficient, ruthlessly brisk women with fine pale English features and a good figure from sitting on horse all day! She had definite opinions on the shape of the world (dreadful), her daughter's marriage (so *fortunate* to have young Cecil in the family), and her daughter's children (not nearly as well behaved as *my* children). She grilled Quinn about her background in a most polite way and almost clapped her hands when she realized that Quinn shared Ian's passion for horses. She did not find it nearly as amusing that the only hunting Quinn had done was with a pellet gun and a boy named Bruce who had been paid a quarter for every pigeon he could knock off the church steeple.

The earl seemed to deal with things by not participating. He grunted through meals and disappeared in the company of Ian with his very own Purdy and Wellingtons to stalk helpless birds. Quinn couldn't help wondering how he'd ever courted his wife. Or what words of wisdom he might have passed on to his sons.

But then on Sunday, on the way back from the services Ian didn't attend, Quinn mentioned how surprised Ian had been to see Blackie down at Hartley Hall, and both mother and father fell into a stricken silence.

"Oh, we thought . . ." the countess began.

"It was so difficult for him, don't you know," the earl offered, his squared florid features strained. "To have to give up the sport. And we couldn't simply sell the beast. He meant too much to the boy."

Lady Malham actually appeared to fight tears. Quinn was astonished by their surprising revelation.

"He was so touched," Quinn said, laying a hand on the older woman's arm, "to know that you were taking such good care of his old friend."

It would be horses, then, that would bridge the distance between Quinn and Ian's mother. The woman really understood what that animal had meant to Ian, couldn't bear the thought of betraying the horse or hurting her son. Quinn met the entreaty in those watery blue eyes and saw deep beneath all that pride and station the helpless pain of a mother for her son, and knew that although they might never agree, they would eventually become friends.

"You said on the way home," Quinn protested.

Ian smiled at her from where he leaned against the doorway to her room. He was in his country clothes—fawn corduroy slacks, tattersall checked shirt, woolen sweater. His cheeks were reddened from the wind off the moors and his hair tumbled from his afternoon ride. Quinn couldn't take her eyes from him. She couldn't slow her heart rate, knowing that he'd want an answer she'd had for three weeks.

"I lied," he answered equably, and stepped inside.

Quinn had been sitting in the armchair by her window, watching the clouds scud across the wild green undulations of Yorkshire. Strung with rock fences, dotted with wind-ravaged trees, sprinkled with sheep. Open and untamed, no matter how long humankind had lived there. A place she truly saw as Ian's.

She turned away from the vista and got to her feet, sliding her hands into the pockets of her skirt. "You're getting awfully bossy, you know that? Is that something I'm going to have to expect from now on?"

He shut the door behind him. "Absolutely."

Quinn's eyebrows raised. "Ian, what is your mother going to say?"

He shrugged. "I told you before. She has no say over who I marry."

"She does about who you corner in one of her bedrooms in the middle of the afternoon."

"Old family tradition," he said with a slow hot smile. "Continuing the family line is very important to us, you know."

She didn't move. She didn't back away, either. "So you've said."

He reached a hand up to the scarf she'd tied beneath the collar of her blouse. "One would be absolutely mortified to find out too late that that couldn't be accomplished."

Quinn wondered where the air in her chest had gone. He seemed to be stealing it with those clever fingers of his as he pulled free the knot in her scarf. "I think we've already tested those waters."

"Not nearly enough since I asked you to marry me."

The scarf pulled loose. Ian stepped a little closer, intent on the buttons discovered beneath.

"Did you?" Quinn asked, facing him.

"Did I what?" His attention was on the first button.

"Ask me to marry you."

Ian's movements slowed. He lifted his gaze to her, and she saw all the heat that had been building up for three weeks while they'd lived five miles apart and conducted clandestine meetings when the prince wasn't looking. She saw the hunger, the need. She saw the fear, and it almost destroyed her.

Still she kept her silence.

"Will you marry me, Quinn?" His hands hadn't dropped. He hadn't stepped away or straightened to attention. All the same, Quinn knew that he'd never been more serious in his life.

Even so, she had to ask. She had to know, because it was important. "What does your family think?" she asked, her voice soft.

Finally losing interest in the buttons, Ian took her by the shoulders.

"I told you," he said, "it doesn't make any difference to me."

"It does to me," she insisted. "That woman will be your children's grandmother. What am I supposed to do if she doesn't want me under her roof?"

Ian's smile was amazed and awed. "You do have some interesting priorities, my love. May I say that I applaud them." He shook his head, still smiling. "You remind her of her mother. Strong and pragmatic. I've told her quite a bit about you, you know. She was especially amazed that you singlehandedly slogged through a bout of malaria with me. She's been an unwilling witness to it."

"Did you like your grandmother?"

Ian didn't even have to think. He didn't really have to answer. It was all there in his eyes. "You two would have been famous together. She tamed the randiest peer in the realm. Did you know that he courted her by singing 'Greensleeves'?"

Quinn tilted her head, even more impressed with her old friend the ghost, who now entertained the new guests under Alistair's wing. "A song I'm particularly fond of," she admitted, anxious now to get on with it. To get past it and back to those buttons. Even so, she hedged. "I don't know," she said. "We haven't consulted Mary beneath a full moon."

Ian snorted unkindly. "We've consulted her every other way imaginable. And don't think she's going to get away with

laughing at His Royal Highness when he cut his finger with th
hedge trimmers.''

"He shouldn't have been playing with them. Besides, I
should be grateful that that was all she did, or those tw
countries might be back at war.''

"He likes you, too.''

"He should. I saved his best bodyguard. And I was the on'
one who knew how to cook the king's favorite dish. I still thin
that couscous was the key to the success of the summit.''

"Don't get cocky, young lady. I'm the Crown employee i
this family, and don't ever forget it.''

Quinn stopped smiling. "Just promise me *you* won't.''

He began rubbing her shoulders. "A copper, that's m
lady. Chief Superintendent Spears-Wykeham at your se
vice.''

"You promise me.''

His eyes softened, darkened. "I promise.''

His words released a smile that came from Quinn's deepe
soul. Down where her dreams had been buried and her hope
had always waited.

"Seem to have lost track of your tradition, there, Giggle
wick,'' she accused, waving a finger at him.

Ian went very still. "This isn't a tradition I'm likely to giv
up again once I've reclaimed it.''

Quinn moved just a little closer, leaned her head back a b
farther so that she could remain face-to-face with Ian. Eye t
eye, toe to toe, close enough to feel the heat rise from his bod
to hear the sudden shudder in his breath.

"I should hope not,'' she answered, lifting her hands to see
their own purchase.

He never took his eyes from hers, the fire that lit them suc
denly hotter, sweeter, bolder. "A tradition that means a grea
deal to me.''

She didn't even look away to see that his fingers had re
turned to her buttons. Her blouse was silk. She was glad she'
worn it, so that she could feel his fingers whisper through i
So he could brush it away from her shoulders and slide it dow
her arms.

"I'm glad,'' she whispered, her blouse all but forgotten fo
the new life in his eyes. "I kind of like it, too.''

"And children?"

Her blouse came free. He swept his hands up over her shoulders and she shuddered with the delicious feel of his calluses. "How many can we fit around the dining-room table?"

The blouse fell. With a rasp of zipper, her skirt followed.

"At least a dozen."

He dipped his mouth to her shoulder and Quinn trembled. His hands spanned her waist. His slacks brushed her legs.

"We'll have to start...soon, then," she managed, her head up, her hands clutching at Ian's back.

He nipped the tender skin of her neck, just below her ear. "Soon," he echoed.

His hand edged upward, toward her breast. His other hand cupped her bottom, fitting her snugly against him so that she had no doubts as to how he felt.

"No boarding schools," she panted.

"Never."

"They'll go to school with the other policemen's kids."

Her knees were giving out. Strange little moans were bubbling in her chest, trying to squeeze past her racing heart. Ian was trailing kisses up her throat.

"Absolutely."

"And horses..."

She couldn't think anymore. He had discovered her breast, his touch sending shafts of light through her. She was whimpering, tugging at his clothes, desperate for the feel of his skin against hers.

"What about horses?" he asked against her ear. He traced the shell with his tongue, and Quinn writhed.

"I don't know," she gasped. "I don't care."

His hand slipped beneath her panties, hot against her skin, intimate and bold. Tormenting, tantalizing. Quinn couldn't stand up.

"Does this mean," he asked, dipping his finger inside and sparking fire, "that you're saying yes?"

Quinn whimpered. She moaned and fought and danced. "Yes," she begged, lifting her face for his kiss. "Yes, yes."

His smile was at once wicked and tender. Possessive, exultant, amazed. Swinging Quinn into his arms, he stepped over to the bed where his grandfather had first courted his grandmother. "In that case," he said, crushing her to him for a kiss, "we'd better get started."

They did. And afterward, holding Quinn in his arms, Ian sang "Greensleeves" to her.

* * * * *

SILHOUETTE®
Desire™

COMING NEXT MONTH

#673 BABY ABOARD—Raye Morgan
Carson James was suave, charming and as far from fatherhood as a man could get. Were Lisa Loring's enticing ways enough to lure him into marriage... and a baby carriage?

#674 A GALLANT GENTLEMAN—Leslie Davis Guccione
Sailing instructor Kay McCormick had one rule for smooth sailing—*never* get involved with club members! But then Jake Bishop and his daughter guided her into the deep waters of love.

#675 HEART'S EASE—Ashley Summers
Valerie Hepburn's tragic past left her feeling undesirable and unattractive. But could persistent businessman Christopher Wyatt persuade Valerie to take a chance on living... and loving?

#676 LINDY AND THE LAW—Karen Leabo
Free-spirited Lindy Shapiro was always getting *into* and *out of* trouble. But Sheriff Thad Halsey wasn't about to let this beauty go... not before apprehending her heart.

#677 RED-HOT SATIN—Carole Buck
Hayley Jerome needed a fiancé fast—her mother was on her way to meet him! Outrageous Nick O'Neill conned his way into playing Mr. Wrong, but he felt very right.

#678 NOT A MARRYING MAN—Dixie Browning
When a silent five-year-old appeared on November's *Man of the Month's* doorstep, secret agent Mac Ford had some questions. But tracking down beautiful Banner Keaton only added to the mystery.

AVAILABLE NOW:

Take 4 bestselling love stories FREE

Plus get a FREE surprise gift!

Silhouette Special Edition

Ahoy, Readers!

Debbie Macomber fires up the engines once again with

NAVY BABY

Torpedoman Chief Riley Murdock looked high and low for the girl he'd fallen in love with during one night of passion. Search as he might, Hannah had vanished into thin air.... Then Riley's commanding officer called him in for a meeting with the navy chaplain. Hannah had surfaced—pregnant—and her preacher father was demanding a wedding....

Be sure to look for Navy Baby (SE #697) in October.

Available in October at your favorite retail outlet, or order your copy now by sending your name, address, zip code or postal code, along with a check or money order for $3.29 (please do not send cash), plus 75¢ postage and handling ($1.00 in Canada), payable to Silhouette Reader Service to:

In the U.S.
3010 Walden Avenue
P.O. Box 1396
Buffalo, NY 14269-1396

In Canada
P.O. Box 609
Fort Erie, Ontario
L2A 5X3

Please specify book title with your order.
Canadian residents add applicable federal and provincial taxes.

SSENBR

SILHOUETTE®
OFFICIAL SWEEPSTAKES RULES

NO PURCHASE NECESSARY

1. To enter, complete an Official Entry Form or 3"× 5" index card by hand-printing, in plain block letters, your complete name, address, phone number and age, and mailing it to: Silhouette Fashion A Whole New You Sweepstakes, P.O. Box 9056, Buffalo, NY 14269-9056.

   No responsibility is assumed for lost, late or misdirected mail. Entries must be sent separately with first class postage affixed, and be received no later than December 31, 1991 for eligibility.

2. Winners will be selected by D.L. Blair, Inc., an independent judging organization whose decisions are final, in random drawings to be held on January 30, 1992 in Blair, NE at 10:00 a.m. from among all eligible entries received.

3. The prizes to be awarded and their approximate retail values are as follows: Grand Prize — A brand-new Ford Explorer 4×4 plus a trip for two (2) to Hawaii, including round-trip air transportation, six (6) nights hotel accommodation, a $1,400 meal/spending money stipend and $2,000 cash toward a new fashion wardrobe (approximate value: $28,000) or $15,000 cash; two (2) Second Prizes — A trip to Hawaii, including round-trip air transportation, six (6) nights hotel accommodation, a $1,400 meal/spending money stipend and $2,000 cash toward a new fashion wardrobe (approximate value: $11,000) or $5,000 cash; three (3) Third Prizes — $2,000 cash toward a new fashion wardrobe. All prizes are valued in U.S. currency. Travel award air transportation is from the commercial airport nearest winner's home. Travel is subject to space and accommodation availability, and must be completed by June 30, 1993. Sweepstakes offer is open to residents of the U.S. and Canada who are 21 years of age or older as of December 31, 1991, except residents of Puerto Rico, employees and immediate family members of Torstar Corp., its affiliates, subsidiaries, and all agencies, entities and persons connected with the use, marketing, or conduct of this sweepstakes. All federal, state, provincial, municipal and local laws apply. Offer void wherever prohibited by law. Taxes and/or duties, applicable registration and licensing fees, are the sole responsibility of the winners. Any litigation within the province of Quebec respecting the conduct and awarding of a prize may be submitted to the Régie des loteries et courses du Québec. All prizes will be awarded; winners will be notified by mail. No substitution of prizes is permitted.

4. Potential winners must sign and return any required Affidavit of Eligibility/Release of Liability within 30 days of notification. In the event of noncompliance within this time period, the prize may be awarded to an alternate winner. Any prize or prize notification returned as undeliverable may result in the awarding of that prize to an alternate winner. By acceptance of their prize, winners consent to use of their names, photographs or their likenesses for purposes of advertising, trade and promotion on behalf of Torstar Corp. without further compensation. Canadian winners must correctly answer a time-limited arithmetical question in order to be awarded a prize.

5. For a list of winners (available after 3/31/92), send a separate stamped, self-addressed envelope to: Silhouette Fashion A Whole New You Sweepstakes, P.O. Box 4665, Blair, NE 68009.

PREMIUM OFFER TERMS
To receive your gift, complete the Offer Certificate according to directions. Be certain to enclose the required number of "Fashion A Whole New You" proofs of product purchase (which are found on the last page of every specially marked "Fashion A Whole New You" Silhouette or Harlequin romance novel). Requests must be received no later than December 31, 1991. Limit: four (4) gifts per name, family, group, organization or address. Items depicted are for illustrative purposes only and may not be exactly as shown. Please allow 6 to 8 weeks for receipt of order. Offer good while quantities of gifts last. In the event an ordered gift is no longer available, you will receive a free, previously unpublished Silhouette or Harlequin book for every proof of purchase you have submitted with your request, plus a refund of the postage and handling charge you have included. Offer good in the U.S. and Canada only.   SLFW·SWPR

SILHOUETTE® OFFICIAL
SWEEPSTAKES ENTRY FORM

4-FWSDS-3

Complete and return this Entry Form immediately – the more entries you submit, the better your chances of winning!

- Entries must be received by **December 31, 1991**.
- A Random draw will take place on **January 30, 1992**.
- No purchase necessary.

Yes, I want to win a FASHION A WHOLE NEW YOU Sensuous and Adventurous prize from Silhouette:

Name _____ Telephone _____ Age _____

Address _____

City _____ State _____ Zip _____

Return Entries to: **Silhouette FASHION A WHOLE NEW YOU,**
P.O. Box 9056, Buffalo, NY 14269-9056   © 1991 Harlequin Enterprises Limited

PREMIUM OFFER

To receive your free gift, send us the required number of proofs-of-purchase from any specially marked FASHION A WHOLE NEW YOU Silhouette or Harlequin Book with the Offer Certificate properly completed, plus a check or money order (do not send cash) to cover postage and handling payable to Silhouette FASHION A WHOLE NEW YOU Offer. We will send you the specified gift.

OFFER CERTIFICATE

Item	A. SENSUAL DESIGNER VANITY BOX COLLECTION (set of 4) (Suggested Retail Price $60.00)	B. ADVENTUROUS TRAVEL COSMETIC CASE SET (set of 3) (Suggested Retail Price $25.00)
# of proofs-of-purchase	18	12
Postage and Handling	$3.50	$2.95
Check one	☐	☐

Name _____

Address _____

City _____ State _____ Zip _____

Mail this certificate, designated number of proofs-of-purchase and check or money order for postage and handling to: **Silhouette FASHION A WHOLE NEW YOU Gift Offer**, P.O. Box 9057, Buffalo, NY 14269-9057. Requests must be received by December 31, 1991.

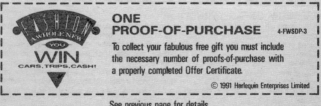

ONE
PROOF-OF-PURCHASE

4-FWSDP-3

To collect your fabulous free gift you must include the necessary number of proofs-of-purchase with a properly completed Offer Certificate.

© 1991 Harlequin Enterprises Limited

See previous page for details.